"I'm sorry I have to say this: I don't love Dick."

"I'm afraid"

"Not for me thanks"

"There's a lot to like about your approach. But,"

"We are not pursuing this."

"I'm overwhelmed"

"No"

"This doesn't sound right"

"Gah!"

Content Notes can be found at the back of the book.

THESE ARE NOT MY FINAL WORDS

SAMANTHA RYAN

For Nex.

This novel contains graphic depictions of suicide and manic depression. Jace and I's stories are similar in that way. The CDC estimates that over 49,000 people died by suicide in 2023. Statistics are even worse among the queer community. If you are experiencing suicidal ideation, there is help available. The Trevor Project has resources and a help line to connect you to an individual who can help. It's never too late. It's never too hopeless. For those who fight this kind of fight, we're in it for the long haul and we can support one another through anything. Keep going. Keep fighting. I'm happy you're here.

- S.

SEASON 1 - EPISODE 1
Pilot

The show starts in the middle of a funeral, I guess.

"Are you okay?"

I heard it more than once that morning and even caught myself saying it a few times. It was such a natural thing to say at a funeral. People wanted to help, but didn't know how. And instead of saying, "Fucking shit, I'm not okay," we all walked around that morning asking each other if *we* were okay, because we knew we weren't. I couldn't tell everyone that the truth was I was numb and had been numb since the day Jace died.

"I'm okay," I had heard Riley tell a young woman earlier who looked like she was crying.

I hadn't spoken to Riley yet.

Nothing I said mattered anyways.

"Jonathan Goodwin," the minister started from the podium, "is going to come and say a few words now."

The church was too silent as I stood and walked up to the front of the open auditorium. My dress shoes echoed in the empty space with each step I took. I avoided looking at Jace's coffin as I climbed the steps to the stage.

"Hi, everyone. I'm Jonathan. If you don't know, Jace and I called each other writing partners, but really that's just a fancy term for creative friends. Together, we created *Dick*. That's the name of our show, which, I know sounds kind of dumb, but it never failed to make us giggle like little kids because we are both actual idiots."

My brain made a mental note of the misuse of 'are' but I tried to ignore it.

"And let me tell you, we both loved *Dick*." I paused to allow the light laughter to brighten the room. "See? It's funny and dumb. He's a little duck and a detective, Dick the dick; it's all really stupid, honestly."

There is no term for when one human is in the present and one is in the past. There's no way to express that one can live while the other can not. No conjugation defined what it meant to survive the death of someone else. The audience looked at me, rows of somber faces, waiting.

"I know you're not supposed to say the word 'suicide' at a funeral for someone who committed suicide, but I know Jace would think that was the funniest shit in the world. So, if you're like me and actually brought your own alcohol to this thing, feel free to join my drinking game and take a swig every time I say the word 'suicide'."

I pulled out a little flask and took a drink as I said it, committing to the bit. Some people laughed. Some people looked at each other, uncomfortable. And others wished they had thought to bring alcohol.

"We met in college. We were both nerds from small high schools studying film because we wanted to be the next Spielberg. When we discovered neither of us had any talent, we decided to become writers."

I paused for the self-aggrandizing laughter that only a room full of writers could produce.

"Then we realized if we became writing partners, we could do twice the work in half the time. Our working partnership was formed out of sheer laziness and procrastination."

More laughter.

I looked back down at my notes and the words started to blur together. I didn't want to do this. I didn't want to do any of this.

"When I came out to Jace, his only response was, 'cool'. And I remember saying, 'That's it?' Like I guess I had kind of expected some half-assed homophobic joke just because he would see the opportunity in front of him. But instead, all I got was a classic, 'cool.' 'That's your only take away?' I remember asking. And he told me that me being gay only meant two things to him. One—that we would never have to fight over girls. And two—that studios would, in his words, 'eat that shit up'. And he was right. We never fought over a single girl and studios loved to be progressive enough to hire a gay writer and his straight partner."

I looked at Riley as I said this and she was laughing with the rest of them, despite the tears on her cheeks.

"I also feel compelled to say this, since he's not here to defend himself, but his name was Jason. His real name was actually Jason. He told me once that anyone in Hollywood could be a Jason—sorry Bateman, I saw you in the crowd earlier —but he told me that only he had the balls to walk around calling himself Jace. Which also was true."

There were scattered murmurs of agreement and I guessed

somewhere in the rows of faces, people were slapping the leg of Jason Bateman who probably grinned in acknowledgement. I don't know. I had never actually met him. Who knows how he was reacting.

"I was the best man in Jace's wedding. When he met Riley, I remember him telling me that he had met the one person in his life who made him whole. Riley is a saint for putting up with all of Jace's hijinks. I guess that seems stupid to say in the face of suicide." I paused and looked around a second before pulling out my flask.

After a quick swig, I continued.

"But Jace, as most of you know, would really do anything for the sake of the bit. I watched him get the police called on him on Hollywood Boulevard at the premiere of *Fantastic Four*. He would have happily gone to jail, too, if it would have made a better punchline. I don't even remember now what the bit was.

"Everything was a joke to Jace and I think we all benefited from that. I know I did. There were times in my career that I was prepared to give up and throw in the towel. Jace was someone who always encouraged me to keep going, keep writing. I'm going to miss that.

"I don't know how to end this, because I feel like this isn't how it's supposed to end. This still doesn't feel like how Jace's story ends." I could hear myself getting quieter as I spoke. The harder I tried to speak up, the closer my voice got to breaking. "Jace was supposed to die of old age. We were going to retire to the Bahamas, because of course we would, and annoy the shit out of Riley. And die when we were old. Of natural causes. Not at thirty-five. From a gun..."

I looked down at my notes. DON'T SAY THE WORD GUN, I had written in large letters.

"I'm sorry," I said, my voice breaking uncontrollably. "I'm

probably going to stop talking now, or they'll ask me to leave. I loved Jace. I wish he knew that. And I'm sure going to miss him. I... thank you..."

I made the mistake of looking at Riley as I made my way back to my seat. I could see her eyes glistening from where I stood. It made my heart ache to see her so broken.

The next person to speak was standing behind the podium and I barely even registered the words they were saying. Each speaker became less and less familiar with the real Jace—like a copy of a copy. I knew it wasn't their fault that he barely showed his actual self to anyone around him, but hearing those stories was like listening to a documentary of someone's life that you didn't know personally. I knew Jace personally. I knew him better than anyone besides Riley.

When everyone had spoken and all final words had been uttered in front of the closed coffin that contained my friend, the family was called to the front of the auditorium for people to file by and pay respects. Riley stood and began making her way to the big black box. The call was for family, but it was really only Riley's family that was present. Jace had no family. Actually, I knew he had a dad he didn't know, and I wasn't sure if the dad even knew what day or time the funeral was.

Riley's mother held her arm as they stood and it was striking to see them next to each other. I had met them once or twice at holidays and forgotten how much Riley looked like her mother, 'only a little less Black' as Jace used to explain to people to drive Riley crazy. She began scanning the front rows until she found me. She waved quickly to usher me forward.

"Oh no," I mumbled, shaking my head.

"Johnny," she mouthed in agitation.

I couldn't refuse her, and made my way to the gaggle of Richardsons. She was jerking her head violently in my direction as I approached and they all kind of laid hands and pushed until I was on the other side. It felt weird, like a violation of their bond somehow, but if Riley wished it, I would oblige.

Person after person filed by with the sad but somber smile that one offers when they are uncomfortable but well wishing. Some of them looked like they had been crying and others glanced solemnly at the shiny death trap behind us before reaching out a hand, as though touching our live bodies would make it better somehow that the dead lingered just out of reach behind us.

I'm so sorry.

Are you okay?

Do you need anything?

I smiled weakly and grasped their hands, thanking them for coming, letting them know it was okay to feel whatever it was that they were feeling.

I couldn't tell them I was feeling nothing—that I had been numb since Jace died and hadn't cried once.

"Johnny," Mark said as he reached out a hand. "Are you okay?"

"Oh...you know," I said, shaking it.

"I'm so sorry."

"Thank you."

"Do you need anything?"

"No," I said, slowly letting my head go back and forth. "Except maybe an extension on the storyboards."

"Listen," he started, "you don't worry about work. It will be there when you're ready. You just take your time."

I nodded, wondering how long I could refuse to work because of Jace's death. He would have loved that. "Thank you."

The reality was, I felt like working was the only thing anchoring my brain at the moment. I had been up until two each morning, writing everything that came into my mind because I couldn't sleep, and the ideas were there. They were probably shit ideas, but I'd sort that part out once I was ready to face Jace's death.

"I'm so sorry for your loss, man," Jason Bateman said as he stood with his hands clasped together.

"Thank you so much," I replied with a nod.

Neither Jace nor I was famous in that sense, but we hung around famous people enough to know that when a famous person was near, it was best to be as cool as possible and say as little as possible. Jace had always been more of a fame whore and loved that he got to work with people who used to be the only ones with blue checks on Twitter, back when it was Twitter and not whatever it was these days.

Jason walked away and I knew it would have given Jace a real hard on to know Bateman had been one of the last to look upon his dead body. I wondered how long it would take for me to stop thinking thoughts in terms of things that Jace would find funny, or weird, or dumb.

When the last person left, we looked at each other expectantly before walking toward the front of the room. I wasn't sure what the next step was. The last week had been a series of getting from one step to another. *Get to Jace's house. Get to the morgue. Get to the funeral home. Get back to Jace's house. Get the suit to the funeral home. Get Riley food. Get some sleep. Get to the church.* I wondered where I had to get to next.

"Are you going to the graveside?" she asked, and I could hear the exhaustion in her voice.

Get to the cemetery.

"Yes, of course."

"Okay, I think we're about to head that way. Where is Blake? I missed him earlier."

"He couldn't make it today."

Her mouth twisted as though she wanted to say something

else but didn't. I didn't have time to get into it with her about how ridiculous it was that my boyfriend wasn't with me at the worst possible moment in my life. It was honestly the last thing I wanted to talk about.

"It's fine," I said instead. "All good."

"Okay, I won't do this now. But we will do this soon," she replied, shaking her head slightly.

"Right," I said, patting my suit pockets. "I forgot my glasses. I'm going to go get them and I'll head that way. Do you need anything?"

"No. Thank you."

She wrapped me in a quick hug before turning to head to her entourage. I moved back to the front of the auditorium and noticed someone sitting up in the front row, staring at the coffin. The top of the head barely reached the back of the pew and for a moment, I thought it might be a child.

"It's over," I said cautiously, unsure who could be waiting. "Are you moving the coffin for the graveside thing?"

The figure didn't move and the closer I got, the more I realized how odd of a shape it was—like too round to be a human head. It was sitting right where I left my glasses. I reasoned it must be something accidentally left on the pew and not an actual person as I kept walking.

But then, it moved.

The closer I got, the more familiar it became.

"What the hell," I mumbled as I realized what I was looking at.

Dick turned around and held up my sunglasses. "Looking for these?"

It was Jace's voice coming from my cartoon duck, staring at me with a little shit grin.

"What the fuck."

"Is that a no?"

"Am I on drugs?" I heard myself ask.

"I wish. That wasn't even real alcohol in that flask."

I closed my eyes and audibly counted to five. When I opened them, Dick was still staring at me with his eyelids drawn comically across half of his eyes. "What the fuck was that? Did you just learn to count or something? Or are you doing that movie thing where you count away your imaginary friend?"

"So you are imaginary."

"Of course I'm imaginary, what the fuck do you think this is? I'm a fucking animated duck. I'm you. Well, I'm Jace. But I'm you." He said it like he was proud.

"I'm having a mental break of some kind. I've lost touch with reality." I slid to the floor of the auditorium and put my head in my hands. "Okay. Thank you. I'm done now. I'll get sleep and take some meds or something. This isn't funny."

"It's *kind* of funny," Dick started, leaning forward to rest his head on the armrest of the pew.

"Why do you look different? Something's different."

He laughed. "I'm drawn art. I'm not used to being presented in three dimensions. I think our brain is filling in some of the gaps maybe."

"That makes sense."

He laughed again. "That's the part that makes sense to you? Jesus Christ."

"I don't have time for this. I've got to go."

I stood and started walking toward the exit. I glanced behind me when after a few steps I realized there was an oversized duck following a couple of feet behind. Whipping around, I looked him eye-to-eye. "Go away."

"Sure thing, asshole. You're the one who made me, so you're the one who is going to make me go away."

"What does that mean?"

"How the fuck should I know? Did I mention the fact that I'm a figment of your own imagination? You're arguing with yourself right now."

I shut my mouth and considered what to say. We were interrupted by four men in suits who approached the coffin methodically.

"Sorry," one of them said abruptly. "We're going to take him to the graveside. Do you need a minute?"

I turned back to where Dick had been standing, but he was gone. "No, I'm good. Thank you."

Silently, I watched them step forward and start their work. They were being quiet, and ignored me as they began unlatching brakes and preparing Jace to move. They didn't know him and hadn't met him before today. Why was Dick here?

I had to go.

I had to go to the cemetery and bury Jace.

I grabbed my sunglasses from the empty pew and headed outside, sliding the glasses on. It felt weird to have a funeral on a day that was so sunny and hot. Funerals were supposed to be overcast, potentially rainy and on a day where one could wrap their heavy wool coats closer to block out the chill of death.

I didn't feel like I was having some kind of mental break with reality, but I wasn't really sure what that would feel like. It had never happened before. The brief thought that Jace would find this *fucking hilarious* crossed my mind.

Everyone else was already gone and I picked up my pace to try and make it to the graveside without being *that guy*. I let myself collapse into the front seat and reached up to adjust the rear-view mirror. As I did, Dick appeared in the backseat, with a grin.

"Oh my god, it's the thing. It's the jump scare from the backseat thing. Jesus, is your whole life one walking cliché?"

"What are you doing in my car?" I yelled.

I turned around but he was gone. When I rotated back, he was in the front seat, reaching over to pull the seatbelt across his animated figure. Except the more I looked, the more I realized the seatbelt he was pulling was also animated. Intrigued, I looked around to see if the regular seatbelt was still there. It was.

"I don't make the rules," Dick huffed, "but I do follow them. Always wear your seatbelt, kid. Safety first, unless there's alcohol. Then it's alcohol first and safety second."

"That's a Jace joke," I said pointedly. "Why would my brain be making a Jace joke in Jace's voice?"

"Why do *you* think you're making Jace jokes in my—or his —whoever's—voice?"

"Well, it is his voice because he voices the character," I objected. "Don't you know that?"

"I don't know anything. Or rather, I only know what you know. And I think we both know that we know that."

"Oh my god." I leaned against the steering wheel. "I can't go to the grave like this."

"You can't *not* go," Dick insisted. "How would that look if you didn't show up?"

"How would it look if you did?!" I yelled back.

"No one else will know I'm there. It's just you that can see me, remember?"

"You're not real," I said, rubbing my hands against my eyes. Slowly I looked to my right and saw Dick grinning as wide as a little duck can grin.

"God damn it."

"Was it an open casket? Because... you know..." he mimicked sticking a gun in his beak and the idea sent a wave of chills down my spine.

"That's not funny."

"Come on, it's a little funny. Jace blew his head off—of course it wasn't an open casket. Oh my god, can you imagine people coming up to pay respects and seeing what was left of his face?"

Dick was laughing so hard he was crying now, small beads of animated tears running down his face before bouncing down to the seat of the car, and I finally understood the phrase 'water off a duck's back'.

"Focus," I reminded myself.

"That's a sick thought," Dick said, regaining his composure. "You're a real sicko."

"Shut. Up."

"My god, do you pitch ideas like this? Don't you ever worry that someone's going to hear your jokes and worry about your own mental health? That's fucking embarrassing, man. How can you even say these things out loud without just being so fucking embarrassed?"

I sighed before turning the music up. If I couldn't get him to go away, at least I could attempt to drown out his noise. The loud beat of Eminem calmed my nerves and as I lost myself to the sound filling the car, I stared straight ahead refusing to acknowledge Dick's presence.

When I pulled up to the cemetery, I looked over to an empty seat. Whatever sort of mental break I was having was luckily short lived. Collecting my thoughts, I took a deep breath before exiting the car.

A small crowd had gathered near the graveside, where an awning loomed over the hole that would eventually consume Jace's body. It gnawed at my mind.

"Are you okay?" Riley asked as I moved close. "You look sick."

"I'm fine," I said, adjusting my sunglasses against the shockingly bright sunlight.

It was supposed to be a small group at the grave, but I didn't even recognize most of them. The service was a quick one. I think at this point Riley was ready to be done.

They lowered the coffin and it seemed to move in slow motion, falling deep into the core of the Earth. When they prepared to move the dirt, they looked at Riley expectantly. She shuffled forward and knelt down before dropping some on top of the coffin. She stood and looked at me, asking with her eyes if I wanted to participate. I didn't, but I also knew this was it.

Stepping forward gently, knowing that all eyes were on me, I grabbed a handful of earth and fell to my knees.

Goodbye, buddy. I'll miss you forever.

I watched the dirt clumps explode upon impact, tarnishing the shine of the expensive container.

And with that, it was over. Jace was gone.

Eventually, everyone left and it was only me and Riley's family.

"Alright," Riley said with arms extended. "I guess we're done."

"Do you need anything?" I asked as I accepted her open embrace.

"No," she said, head buried into my neck. "I don't know what's next, you know?"

"Yeah," I agreed. I didn't know either.

It had all fallen apart so quickly. I didn't know which piece to start with to even attempt to fix it.

"*Now* will you tell me where Blake is?" she asked, wiping her nose.

"I don't even know," I replied honestly.

She pulled away and opened her mouth to say something, but stopped herself. "Call me tomorrow. Okay?"

"Yeah. Of course. Your family is still here for a while, right?"

"Yeah, my mom will be here for a week or so."

"That's good."

"Okay."

"Okay."

I watched her walk back to her family and they all hugged as they moved away. My eyes trailed back down to the freshly settled dirt that covered Jace's body. I kicked my foot at the dirt. It was time to go.

The house was empty when I got back. I slipped my shoes off by the door before heading to the bar cart. I was really trying to cut back on my drinking for obvious reasons, but I felt a day like today was one of the very specific occasions that called for a little something.

I brought my knuckle of scotch to the couch and plopped down. Time passed, though I didn't notice until the front door opened. Blake moved to turn on a few more lights and watched me carefully.

"Hey, you okay?"

"Yeah, thanks. How are you?"

It sounded as hollow as I felt. He didn't answer and instead moved into the kitchen to get a drink before coming back and sitting opposite from me.

"Are you sleeping here tonight?" I asked.

"We don't have to do this now," he said quietly, smoothing an imaginary wrinkle on his pants.

"Might as well," I said before taking another sip.

He didn't want to admit that he knew it was over before Jace killed himself—that he had been sleeping at his new boyfriend's house weeks before I told him my best friend had died. And if I wanted to, there was likely an option in which I could guilt him with my grief to stay with me.

"I didn't want it to be this way."

I wished I could laugh, but I couldn't. "Yeah, obviously. Or do you mean specifically in the wake of someone's death?"

"I don't want to pile onto your pain."

"I know. I actually believe that. Sometimes things just don't work out."

We sat there, in silence, I think both afraid that saying anything else would make it hurt more than it already did. I didn't really have anything else to say. I had known for a while that Blake wasn't the love of my life. In fact, there were times when he was gone for work that I relished the idea of being alone in the house. I was self-aware enough to know that when you dread the return of your partner to your shared space, it was likely a sign that they shouldn't continue to be your partner.

I wasn't even that mad when I found out about the boyfriend. In some funny way it was even more relief that he too didn't want to commit to this. I don't know what kept me from breaking up with him or vice versa, but in the moment, after the loss of Jace, I knew it was time to say goodbye for good.

At the same time, I really didn't want to be alone. And I didn't want to admit to him that I didn't want to be alone. So instead, I let him go.

"I can get my things out this weekend."

"It's whatever."

"I'll always be here if you need it, you know that. We can still be in each other's lives."

It was nice to think about—this idea that people you collected in your life would always be there, even if it wasn't in the way you originally thought. But the reality was Blake and I had less and less in common every day and after he moved his stuff out of the house, we'd likely never see each other again. He had always been jealous of my relationship with Jace—that much I knew.

"I don't think you should be here alone," he offered as he stood. "Do you want me to stay tonight?"

"What, you think I'm going to kill myself too? I'm not that dramatic. I'll be fine."

The truth was, for the first time in a long time, I thought I could get some sleep. I had hardly slept since Jace died, but now, with him deep in the ground and nothing else left to do, there was a part of me that felt like I could get some rest and peace. I wasn't going to kill myself. I certainly wasn't going to let Jace kill me.

He moved upstairs to get more of his things and I finished my scotch as I heard him rummaging around through our life, pulling the little pieces he wanted to take with him into his new future. My things would remain here, frozen in our shared past.

I shifted on the couch, resting my head against one of the pillows. From the vantage point, I could see a photo of myself, Jace, and Riley in Mexico. We had gone after *Dick* was optioned, which in hindsight was not the point at which we should have been celebrating, but we were stupid and excited. Jace looked happy in the photo with his arms wrapped around Riley's face and I had to believe that all of that was just as real for him as it was for me.

When you look back on a life post-mortem and search desperately for clues of suffering, you'll find them. The lines of reality were beginning to blur and it was getting harder for me to know who Jace really was at any given moment. But then, at a resort in Mexico, we were happy. *Weren't we?*

Blake didn't say anything when he left, silently drifted through the house and out the door for good. I was still horizontal on the couch and was trying not to get too excited about the realization that I was falling in and out of sleep, when I heard a noise.

I opened my eyes wide enough to see what was causing the

problem and was staring straight at Dick, settling his feathers into the chair where Blake had been sitting only an hour before.

"What the fuck."

"What?" he asked, flicking his tail back and forth rapidly like a real duck. "I'm trying to get comfortable."

"Don't get comfortable. You're not fucking real. Go away."

"If you want me to go away, make me go away. I don't know how many times I have to remind us of this, but I'm part of your imagination. I go when you say I go."

"THEN GO," I huffed.

"Nah-ah."

I heard his little feathers ruffle again as he continued to shake his head back and forth.

"It's not that simple. You can't just say the words. You have to mean it. You gotta believe it, buddy."

My eyes shot open at the use of 'buddy'. Jace called me that all the time and hearing him say it made it seem so real.

"This isn't funny anymore," I said, sitting up to face the duck head on. "This is fucking twisted and I want it to stop. You're not Jace. Go away."

He shrugged as much as a duck can shrug. "I never said I was Jace. You're the one who gave me his voice. Do we want to talk about that?"

"He voiced Dick. It wasn't my decision."

"Because you didn't want him to. Right?"

"Shut up."

"But you didn't. You knew how dangerous it was for either of you to be attached to *Dick* in that way. In fact, you thought Jace was going to leave after the first season, didn't you? You thought that all the time. Remember that?"

I did remember. But anyone who had an objective view of the strange and often erratic behaviors of Jason Van Noy would agree that keeping barriers in place for the survival of the show was necessary.

Whether it was my actual responsibility or a self-imposed one, someone needed to be in control of all the production decisions that had to be made regarding *Dick*. And it worked for us that I was the person with Excel sheets and Jace was the one having drinks with a director in a seedy bar in West Hollywood.

"So, what now? What do we do? Because I need to get some sleep and you need to leave."

"You can get some sleep. Who said you couldn't get some sleep?"

I closed my eyes on the couch and wiggled around trying to make myself comfortable despite the funeral clothes I was still wearing. When I settled down, I could feel cartoon eyes boring into my soul.

Turning my head, I opened my eyes and was staring straight into the little round bulbs of Dick's animated black eyes. He had one wing on each cheek, cradling his head delicately as he stared, leaning against the couch.

"Jesus-fucking-Christ."

"Maybe get out of that suit, you psychopath. Wouldn't you be more comfortable in some shorts or something?"

He wasn't wrong. *I wasn't wrong.*

I pulled myself out of the couch and headed upstairs to change. He followed behind, hopping along, flapping his wings and talking non-stop.

"Am I really this annoying?" I asked.

"Excuse you. And yes."

"Then why can't I tell myself to shut up?"

"Go ahead," he challenged.

I stopped at the top of the stairs and we looked at each other a few minutes before I headed on toward the bedroom.

My brain barely registered the things that were missing that Blake had taken, which I guessed I should have shown me how separate our lives had already become.

Once changed, I headed to the bed and collapsed into it. I pulled my phone out of my pocket and saw the messages that had accumulated throughout the day that I had been ignoring. It was nice, certainly, to see physical representations of how much those around me cared. It was also slightly stressful to know I was going to have to respond to all of them.

I opened the latest one—a production assistant from *Dick*. *Thinking of you today and sending thoughts and prayers.*

Thoughts and prayers.

Closing the messages, I looked at a few of my social media tags. People I didn't even know were tagging me in stories of Jace's death. A few of them even accused me of being involved somehow.

How could @J_Goodwin not see how much @JaceoffXXX was suffering? #WTF.

I let my phone fall to the bed next to me and listened to the silence of the room. I didn't have an answer for anyone, really.

"You know," Dick said, lying on his side with one wing propped under his head, "if this was the end of the episode, it would have some kind of cliffhanger. Like some kind of revelation, like maybe you killed Jace. Did you kill Jace?"

"You know I didn't."

"But the audience doesn't…"

"There is no audience," I said, rolling over.

"Or is there?"

"There isn't. And since it's the end of episode one it wouldn't be a revelation, it would be foreshadowing. You'd want to plant the idea in the mind of the audience here that I killed Jace without saying it so blatantly."

"You never were good at writing mysteries."

"I know," I admitted, closing my eyes.

2

SEASON 1 - EPISODE 2
An Anti-Hero's Journey

I didn't feel like I slept, but I wasn't really sure I was fully awake. It all began to blur together in a timeless void.

"Are you awake?" Dick asked, next to me in the bed.

"Yeah," I said out loud.

"Are you going to get up?"

"Yeah."

I rubbed my eyes and looked at the clock. Turns out, I hadn't slept a bit.

"What are we doing today?"

"*We* are doing nothing. *I* am going to work."

"Really?" he asked, hopping up and jumping lightly on the bed.

The sun was filtering through the window and I marveled

at how it appeared to illuminate his body as he jumped. As though he was real.

"Why can't I go with you?"

"Because you aren't real," I reminded myself, rolling out of the bed and heading toward the bathroom.

He was sitting on the sink when I got there, looking at his reflection in the mirror.

"I look pretty real," he huffed as I got ready. I checked my phone again before heading downstairs. It occurred to me that I was looking because I was expecting a morning text from Jace. It normally came in the form of a, *morning mother fucker.*

The idea brought a smile to my face as I got in my car. Dick appeared in the passenger's seat as soon as I shut my door. The motions from the day before played through my head and I turned on my favorite Eminem playlist before backing out of my driveway.

My plan worked, at least momentarily, as Dick disappeared until I walked up to the door of my production company. As I pushed the door open, he shuffled past me into the lobby like he owned the place. When I entered, people turned to watch. Their stares were so intense that for a brief moment I thought maybe they could see Dick too.

Annie met me at the door to my office and looked like she had just found out Jace died that day.

"Johnny," she said softly. "Are you okay?"

"Yeah," I said, pulling my bag over the top of my head. "I'll pick up where we left off. I'll catch up."

"Really, you should take a few more days. Nothing bad will happen while you're gone."

That seemed like a strangely suspicious way of trying to calm me, but I let it go.

"I'm totally fine. If I'm home, I'm sitting in an empty house. I'd rather be here working and doing something."

She looked like she wasn't sure how to stop me and instead silently followed me into my office as I walked. The sad smiles and looks of concern hadn't bothered me at the funeral, because of course everyone looks like that at a funeral, but here it seemed so out of place and haunting that it started to rattle my nerves. How long were those looks going to last?

"Jesus Christ," Dick muttered, looking around as he walked up. "Who died?"

Before I could look down I heard him collapse into a pile of sarcastic laughter. It was terrible, but I did smile before I could stop it. When I turned to Annie, who was still waiting near the door of my office, she looked concerned.

"If you need anything at any time, let me know, okay?"

"Sure."

"Can I get you a coffee or something?"

"Yeah, actually, that would be great."

I rubbed my hands over my eyes as she left and sat in the chair. My emails were piling up and I had revisions I needed to go over, but everything felt like it was out of reach from my brain.

Opening my bag, I pulled out my glasses and turned on my laptop. As I did, I looked down at a note that had Jace's handwriting on it. It was a note about a payroll thing he had asked me the week before he died. I still needed to do that. At least now I wouldn't have to explain the answer to him.

I stared at the computer screen and nothing was going through my brain. Instead, I was suddenly acutely aware that Jace's office next to mine was empty. It being empty in itself wasn't that unusual. Toward the end, Jace was rarely in the office. He never attended our staff meetings and, as I could see in hindsight, was straight up unpredictable when he was inside, setting everyone on edge. I think in that sense, it just made it easier for everyone to encourage him to do his own thing without being in the office and bothering the rest of us.

But now, the office was empty and always would be. I guessed that Riley would want some of his stuff. I stood up and grabbed a box on the floor as I headed toward Jace's office.

"What are you doing?" Dick asked, rushing after me.

"I'm cleaning out his office," I mumbled once I was assured that no one else was close enough to hear me talking to my imaginary friend.

"You can't do that," he insisted.

"Why not?"

"It's not your stuff. That's a violation."

"For who?" I asked as I put the box on top of Jace's desk.

Piles of paper littered the desk—some as old as the beginning of season one. There were countless doodles on every paper I saw and it brought a smile to my face.

Cautiously, I opened the drawers and saw the stuff that was likely put there by Annie because it was way too organized for anything Jace had ever done in his life. There were piles of pens and some candy—that part was definitely Jace. My eyes fell on a half empty bottle of whiskey.

"No way!" Dick exclaimed. "It's me!"

He pointed to a little miniature rubber duck. I had gotten it for Jace as a joke, years ago. Once *Dick* was in production, we had started buying little ducks to annoy each other until it got to the point where other people were buying us ducks too, and we realized very quickly we couldn't keep buying ducks every time we saw one. But this was one of the original ducks and I had no idea Jace kept it in his desk the whole time.

"Yeah," I said, picking it up. "You were always everywhere for us. We saw you in everything we did."

"And I see you in everything I do, too."

I snickered as I held the little duck in my hand, analyzing

each little piece of it as though maybe it held some kind of clue that I missed, before letting it fall from my hands into the box. As it did, my eye fell on an envelope on the desk that looked important. I picked it up and looked at the sender—it was a law office. I started to open it when my eyes caught movement at the door.

At the same moment I looked up, I casually set the envelope in the box. Annie watched me, eyes filled to the brim with concern.

"What are you doing?"

"Cleaning stuff out," I said simply. I was immediately very conscious of the idea that everyone around me both looked like they were about to cry at any minute, but also were waiting for me to cry at any minute, and I wasn't sure how to handle either of those ideas.

"You don't have to do this. Let me do it."

"Nah," I reassured. "I think it's very therapeutic. Maybe."

Dick laughed.

She moved closer and handed over the cup of coffee. "Who were you talking to?"

"What?" I asked as I accepted the mug.

"You were talking before I came in. Who were you talking to?"

"Oh, well, you know," I said, trying to think up something, "I still... geez, this is embarrassing, but I think sometimes I still kind of talk to Jace, I guess."

It wasn't a *complete* lie, since I was actually talking to Jace, as Dick, who was really me.

"Oh," she said quietly. "I'm sorry. That probably does help. I'm sorry I asked."

"No, it's fine." I said, taking another loud sip. "Maybe we just keep this to ourselves, though?"

"Of course. I'll be in my office if you need anything."

"Thanks," I said with a tight smile before she left.

"This is getting depressing," Dick commented, looking back down into the drawer.

"You know, for once I agree with you."

I rushed to pull the remaining items out of the drawer and shove them into the box. All the little pieces of Jace's life would be contained in boxes from now on. His clothes packed away and likely donated, if I had a guess on what Riley was doing to their house.

Standing, I pulled the heavy cardboard close and turned the lights out as I left. I sat back at my desk and watched people walking back and forth in the hallway. I wasn't zoning out on purpose, but it felt like I wasn't even the one in control anymore. Like life was happening and I was participating only as an estranged witness from afar.

"Are you okay?" Annie asked, appearing in the doorway.

"Yeah, sorry, must have zoned out."

"I'm leaving; are you going to stay long?"

"Taking a half day?" I asked with as much joy as I could muster.

"Very funny," she said, until she realized I was being serious and her eyebrows wrinkled. "It's four o'clock."

"What?" I asked, sitting up and looking at the phone on my desk. I had five missed calls and a million texts, along with dozens of app notifications. The little clock indicated it was a few minutes after four.

She moved inside the office and shut the door. "I'm really worried about you."

"I'm fine."

"I think you're still... going through a lot. Which is totally normal. But I think you should see someone."

"I don't need to see someone. I'm fine. Really. I'm grateful for you looking out for me, but I'll be okay."

She looked at me like she didn't believe me, but wasn't sure what else she could offer.

"Why don't you and Blake get away for a while? Take a vacation?"

Dick laughed from under the desk.

"Actually, we, uh, broke up."

I regretted the words as soon as they came out of my mouth. The concern on Annie's face went from present to severe and immediately I could see the calculations starting.

"Oh my god, Johnny, I'm sorry. Why don't you come over for a bit? We could watch a movie or something?"

I smiled and enjoyed the fact that it was genuine. "Really, Annie, I'm okay. I know I'm tired from everything the last week, but I'll be fine. I promise. If I need anything at all, I'll call you."

Her mouth shifted into a thin line and she turned toward the door. As she opened it, she swiveled to offer her final thoughts. "You know it's okay to not be okay, right? After my mom died, I was a mess. For months. And I know there's nothing I can say to make you feel better, but if you want someone to listen to you, please call me."

I stood up and moved around the desk to offer a hug. She leaned her little frame into my arms. "Thank you."

She smiled up at me with tears in her eyes before she walked away. I still hadn't cried. I wondered why as I watched her leave, pulling out her cell phone as she did. I think I always thought I would cry if Jace died. In fact, I assumed I'd be an absolute wreck. But I hadn't. Instead, I just felt numb. Maybe I had died too, and Jace didn't tell me.

"Let's go home," Dick said next to me, reaching his feathers up to grab my hand.

I could feel it, or thought I did. There was texture and softness rubbing against my fingers as he gripped them.

"Alright. Let me get our things."

I moved back around, grabbing my bag and my eyes fell to the box on the floor. Riley would want it. Bracing myself, I hoisted it up and headed outside to the car. Dick plodded along behind me in silence.

The talking was annoying, but the silence was somehow worse.

"Do you have memories?" I asked, once we were in the car.

"I guess?" he replied, looking confused.

"What's your earliest memory?"

"Our seventh birthday party."

I smiled. "That was a good one."

"You got a bicycle and your friends spent the night. We watched movies and stayed up late. And when your parents went to sleep you watched *Candyman* even though you weren't allowed to."

Remembering it made me laugh. I had nightmares for weeks afterwards. I had completely forgotten all of it, like it was locked in some little vault in my brain.

The house was as empty as expected. None of the food in my fridge looked good. None of the movies on Netflix looked interesting. Nothing held any interest to me whatsoever. I sat at the couch with a glass of whiskey and opened my laptop, watching the cursor blink over and over.

"What are you writing?" Dick asked from behind, pouring himself a whiskey on the rocks.

"I don't even know anymore. Ideas that don't have meaning."

I closed the laptop before he could read any of the jibberish on the page.

It was time to go to bed, or at least go and lie in the bed and stare at the ceiling until it was time to get up and go to work. No beginning, no end, a pattern of moments to convince those around me I was alive. Motions to indicate active brainwaves. Mirroring behaviors to simulate living. None of it was real, though. Maybe I really was dead. How could I even know anymore?

"We brought in a grief counselor," Mark said slowly, causing me to snap to attention at his face in front of mine.

I was in Mark's office. At work. Not at home. Not in bed.

I wasn't sure if he was talking slowly for my benefit or just because he wasn't sure if he was saying all the right things in the right order. Mark leaned against his desk, sitting his butt on the edge of it like a concerned college professor trying to convince me that midterms were equally as important as anything else in the syllabus.

"Okay."

"And we think maybe you should see them."

I looked from Mark to Annie and pointed to my chest. "You think I should see the grief counselor?"

"We're really worried about you," Annie said gently, leaning forward in the chair next to me. She reached out her hand and touched my knee.

Dick was practically rolling on the floor behind her, laughing. I wanted to tell him to shut up, but didn't. Or rather couldn't. Because yelling shut up at an animated duck that only I could see would have them calling someone other than a grief counselor.

"I'm fine," I said instead, lifting a leg over the other and sliding further down in the overstuffed chair.

"Right, we know, but it's just a lot to think about anyone going through what you went through and maybe it would be good to see someone. It couldn't hurt, right?"

"You've done it now!" Dick yelled, his wings spread wide on the floor next to him as though he was making a snow angel in the carpet.

"Okay," I conceded. "I'll talk to them."

"They're in Oak."

"What? Now?" I asked, my stomach filling with dread at the realization. I didn't mind talking to someone, but I had to be prepared for it first. I had to have my set down.

"Yeah, she can see you now, if that works," Annie offered with a smile.

I wanted to say no and tell them that, really, I was fine and everything was fine and maybe even better than fine, that my life had gotten better since Jace died, minus the animated duck that was following me around that served as a constant reminder of what my life had been before Jace died, even though it wasn't really about Jace or me it was just some imaginary manifestation of something I had created with Jace and oh my god I needed to see the grief counselor.

"I'll go now."

I headed upstairs to Oak and ignored the faces of the people passing me. Since being in the studio AJD (After Jace's Death) people gave me a variety of looks in passing that equated to awkward support or general sympathy. BJD (Before Jace's Death) the looks were generally ones of pure adoration directed at Jace. He was the often the light of the room, captivating any audience he could find.

There was someone waiting in one of the chairs outside and their eyes got wide when they saw me approach. They stood as I got near and hurried off without a word. I got it; why would you want to follow the main act? I sat in the chair they had abandoned and only then realized that Dick was plodding behind me step-by-step.

He climbed up into the chair next to me and pulled out a magazine from an undisclosed location behind his back. I wished for a brief moment that I could experience that kind of cartoon life where I could manifest the exact thing needed from behind my back whenever I wanted.

I watched his little webbed feet flip back and forth like a toddler waiting at the doctor's office.

"What?" he quacked.

I wondered how much control I had over his movements. Focusing all my energy, I tried to make him slap his own face. He turned his beak toward me, eyes squinting as he realized I was up to something. We continued in a beady-eyed face-off until the door next to me opened and I remembered I was a grown adult sitting by myself at my place of employment. Someone I vaguely remembered from the art department stepped out from the conference room. They had clearly been crying.

"Please call me if you need anything."

I watched the art department girl lift her tissue to her nose before nodding and walking away. She didn't look down at me as she did. It was hard for me to wrap my brain around the idea that she was likely crying over Jace. Did she know him? Could he have picked her out of a lineup if needed? How could she be so upset over him and I hadn't felt anything for days?

"Johnny. Hi there. I was hoping you'd stop by today."

"Really?" I asked, stuffing my hands in my pockets awkwardly.

Dick hopped up from the chair and pushed forward with one wing raised out in front of him like he was a linebacker.

"Yes. I think we could spend some useful time together."

"Sure."

"I'm Meredith Clark."

"Johnny Goodwin, but you know that, I think."

I followed her into the conference room and sat at one of the empty chairs. She sat opposite me and smiled warmly.

"Before we begin, anything that you say or feel in here is

valid. There's no wrong way to grieve someone. And grief can manifest itself in all kinds of ways."

Without thinking about it, I glanced toward Dick who was standing with one wing over his chest as though pledging allegiance to the flag.

"Sure."

"If you want to talk, we can. Or if you want to cry, you can. Even if you just want to sit in silence and do nothing, sometimes that can help too."

I sat for a second considering if I had anything worth saying. "I haven't cried once since Jace died. Is that weird?"

"No," she said as though it was obvious, "that isn't. You might have it hit you all at once later. You might not have fully processed everything."

"How can I process everything?"

"You will, over time. Talking it through helps, certainly."

I saw a light bulb come on over Dick's head before he reached out with a bat and smashed it, sending imaginary shards all over the floor.

"You want to get rid of me?" he yelled from below.

"Yes," I said, turning to the counselor. "I need to process everything to clean out my brain—dump it of all the things I'm holding on to. How do I do that?"

"There are many ways. You could try writing a letter to express your thoughts?"

"Yeah, maybe."

"Are you sleeping?"

"Not really," I admitted.

"That's also very common. If you need to, there's nothing wrong with seeing a doctor who can prescribe a little help for that right now."

"Yeah, I guess."

"Are you having any thoughts of self-harm?"

I laughed even though I knew I shouldn't. Dick laughed too.

"No."

"Why is that funny?"

"Because clearly I'm not the one that people should have been asking. I've never once thought about killing myself. In fact, it's so hard for me to even understand what was going on with Jace then. Toward the end I mean. Like, it doesn't make sense."

"Do you think you need it to make sense to you?"

"I guess not... but, maybe? Yeah?"

I looked at her outfit. It was professional, without being designer or flashy and I wondered how much time she spent analyzing choices she made, like which shade of taupe was the most disarming for people in distress, or whether or not it was time to retire her salt and pepper feathered bangs she'd probably had since the seventies. It was coming back though, as everything did, so maybe she was just desperately holding on until she could feel a connection again to those around her through her fringe.

"Johnny?"

"What?"

"I asked if you were angry."

I shook my head slowly. "I'm not anything."

"Why do you think that is?"

"I have no idea," I answered honestly.

"You really have no idea?" Dick asked at my feet.

Before I could stop myself, I looked down at him to glare and Meredith pulled back from the table to see what I was looking at.

"Are you alright?"

I nodded quickly.

"Do you still talk to Jace?"

I smiled, amused that Annie had told on me. "Yeah, I guess I do."

"Does it help?"

"No, it's really annoying, actually."

"Hey," Dick protested under me, slapping desperately against my shins.

"How is it annoying?"

"Because I want it to go away. I want to get rid of him." I switched one leg across the other and heard Dick quack wildly on the floor.

"Of Jace?" she asked.

I nodded. "Like, let's say I hear him talking to me maybe? How would I get rid of that?"

"Talking to you?" She leaned forward.

"Yeah, like if I heard his voice in my head. Like arguing with me? Or like my subconscious maybe?"

"Do you hear him now?"

"Do you?" Dick asked, suddenly right behind Meredith.

"No," I lied.

"How often are you hearing him?"

"Not all the time. Are those coloring books?" I asked, pointing to a pile of books on the table.

"Yes. Are you trying to deflect?"

"No, I'm curious about the coloring books. Do you therapize kids?"

"No. I'm a grief counselor, not a therapist. Is that another deflection?"

"For fuck's sake," Dick whispered, falling to his back.

"No," I said simply.

"Sometimes," she started, "it helps adults to have something to do with their hands or their mind before they start to speak. There's no right or wrong way to do therapy."

"Can I color?" I asked.

She nodded. "Crayons are under your seat."

I reached down and around, fishing for the tools. Dick rolled slightly to kick his little webbed foot against the back, pushing the bucket my way. As soon as my fingers made contact with the cold plastic, I pulled and set the container on the top of the table.

"I always enjoyed coloring as a kid. There was something calming about filling a page with carefully placed color."

"A therapist might suggest that's an indication for your desire to control the world around you."

"Good thing you're not a therapist then."

She smiled.

"I know I love controlling the world around me. I've never not known that. Jace knew it and didn't mind it. That's why we worked so well together. There were times when I didn't mind if he was in control. But other times, he stepped back and let me deal with it all."

"What was your relationship with Jace like?"

"Jesus," I started, carefully edging my green crayon across the leaf. "I don't know. We were friends. Co-workers. Spent all our time together? It was good, I guess? All good."

"Are you being honest?"

"Yeah, tell her what you told me," Dick said.

"Tell you what?"

"About Jace. And you. Or me—really us."

"What?" the counselor asked, now confused.

"Nothing," I said, shutting down completely. "There is nothing to tell. There was nothing like that between us."

I continued to color and watched the streaks of green fill the little spaces in the page, nice and neat. Each little piece of pigment right where it was supposed to go, as though it always belonged there in the first place.

3

SEASON 1 - EPISODE 3
Clip Show

The noise of the restaurant added to my already mounting anxiety while I debated what to drink. I looked up from the menu and saw Jace scanning the room trying to find me. I motioned him over and he grinned as he sat down.

"What's the special occasion?" I asked before he pulled his menu closer and reached out to smooth the iron-pressed black tablecloth in front of him.

"No occasion, I just wanted to catch up with you. It feels like it's been years since we've sat and talked."

"Whose fault is that?" I leaned back in my chair.

He laughed lightly and shook his head as though brushing it off. His bright eyes were focused on the words in front of him and I noticed his hair was shorter than last time I saw him and his stubble was contained in a way that made him look presentable.

"You look all cleaned up, too. This *must* be serious."

He glanced up this time, still smiling, though his eyes betrayed him.

"Are you breaking up with me?" I asked dramatically as the waiter came over.

"Good evening, gentlemen," they said with a smile. "Have you dined with us before?"

"No," Jace said, still scanning the drink menu.

"Tonight we have a few specials..."

The waiter continued their practiced speech, pausing to point down at my menu and I forced myself to look up and watch the entire thing since Jace had his head buried.

"Whiskey on the rocks for me. Splash of water."

"Same," Jace said, finally looking up at him.

As the waiter left, Jace leaned forward across the table, shuffling the accouterments sprinkled around. "How are you doing?"

I laughed and tapped my fingers on the tabletop. "Would you stop? You call me up and ask me to meet you for dinner at a place way too fancy for the two of us and you want to start with 'how are you doing?' Why are you being so weird? Is it about *Dick*? Have we been canceled already?"

He raised his hands in defense. "Okay, okay. Sorry. Nothing is wrong. I'm nervous. To talk to you."

"Jason Van Noy, you lie."

"I want your advice. About Riley. I think I'm going to propose."

My eyebrows shot up at the news. "Really? About time. What do you need my advice for?"

He hesitated and his grin slipped slightly. "You know I'm, like, never hesitant about decisions. I'm a feet-first guy."

"Always."

"But like I feel like I'm kind of dragging my feet here and I'm not sure why. I know, my parents were divorced and it was awful. Maybe we don't even need to get married. We're having fun as it is, why change that?"

"Has she brought it up?"

"Several times. Like we might be on the verge of an ultimatum kind of situation here."

I considered his words carefully as the waiter set our glasses on the table. It was no secret to me Riley wanted to get married. But part of me worried about forcing Jace into a situation he didn't want to be in. There was no future in my eyes where Jace got married because he thought he had to and then stayed when that changed later. He was someone who had always done exactly what he wanted when he wanted.

"Alright," I started. "Pro and con time. Pro?"

"I like her."

"That's a good start." I took a drink of my whiskey.

"I thought so. She makes me laugh."

"Also important. What else?"

He sipped on his own drink. "It's what you do, right? When you love someone? You either get married or you break up?"

"Sure," I hedged. "I mean, I don't think everyone just *has* to get married. But if you want to and she wants to, you should."

He nodded, slowly.

"You love her?"

"I do."

"Then, yeah," I started, "if you love her and everything is hinging on her wanting to get married then you should probably propose."

"I love you and I've never felt compelled to propose to you. And you'd never give me an ultimatum to marry you or get the fuck out."

I laughed and ignored the flutter in my chest. "You're not *in love* with me; there's actually a difference, you sociopath. If you're *in love* with her then you should propose."

"Is there though? A difference, I mean."

I stopped smiling and picked up my glass, frantically looking for something for my hands to do.

"Yeah, Jace, there is."

"But you *are* in love with me, aren't you?"

"You wish," I shot back. "Most days I don't even like you."

He snorted and raised his glass before mumbling, "We both know that's not true."

"We're getting off topic. Are there any cons?"

He leaned back. "Do I like her enough to spend every minute of every day with her?"

"Do you?"

"I think so," he offered, running a finger around the rim of his glass.

"...but?"

"Marriage is such a," he paused, "... thing. You know? Like we have fun now, sure, but what about ten years from now? Twenty years from now?"

"I mean, she's stayed with your dumb ass so far."

"That's true. And I didn't think anyone but you could do that. "

We both knew he wasn't talking about her being the one that would leave. "What other cons are there?"

"I don't know."

"Look at it this way, if you didn't propose and she broke up with you tomorrow, how would you feel?"

"Devastated."

"Then I think that's your answer."

He nodded slowly, leaning back and pushing the feet of the chair up in a way that no one in the history of the restaurant would have dared. "You sick son-of-a-bitch, you're right. See? This is what I needed. I needed the back and forth to think it out."

"That is my real purpose in life, Jace, to help you sort out your scary man feelings. Do you have a ring?"

"No," he said. "That's the other part of my ask here tonight. I was thinking, would it be weird for you to try and figure out what kind she likes?"

"I can try, but you know I'm the worst at keeping secrets."

He laughed loudly. "I know. I think she probably already knows. But if you ask, at least I know she'll like it. Plus that's me putting in effort, right?"

I narrowed my eyes. "Riley sure is lucky to have found you."

We were interrupted by the waiter, back to give more information and take our food order. This time, Jace was relaxed, having unburdened his soul on me. I wasn't even hungry anymore.

"A salad?" Jace asked when the waiter left. "You're not doing vegan again, are you?"

I shook my head. "Not quite."

"You need to eat more than just salads," he huffed as he emptied his glass.

I was tempted to poke him about him eating more than liquid calories, but held my tongue.

"Salads are healthy. I'm trying to be healthy."

"It's so much work," he complained, leaning back in his chair. "We've still got a little time before we have to worry about that. We're still young, right?"

"Back to Riley. I say green light."

"Then I guess I should go for it. If there's no other reasons why I shouldn't."

I shrugged. "I like Riley a lot. She fits in with your life and we always have fun together."

He paused like he was thinking of something else.

"What?" I asked, pushing my fork back and forth.

"It's not like anything has to change, I guess," he offered.

"No," I reassured. "Of course not."

There was no reason why him telling me about Riley should have made him uncomfortable. I wondered if he thought I would object somehow or be jealous? I knew I never occupied that much space in his life and eventually he would have someone who did. If that person was Riley, I was happy. She was kind and funny and overall made him a better person. That's what everyone wanted out of life, right? For their friends?

"Why didn't you tell him?" Dick asked.

I looked over at the duck, sitting at the table as close to me as he could possibly get.

"You weren't there."

The memory was beginning to feel hazy and Jace watched me carefully. "Are you okay?"

That never happened.

"I feel like if you just told him, he would have understood."

"What good would that do? It doesn't matter anyways."

"What doesn't matter?" Jace asked. "What are you talking about?"

He never asked that. *That wasn't how it happened.*

"What happened was, he left you that night and proposed to Riley. And they got married and lived happily ever after."

"Shut up," I started. "That's actually not what happened. They didn't live happily ever after. He killed himself."

"Who killed himself?" Jace asked, looking around. "Are you okay?"

But it wasn't a memory? A dream?

"Just think about what would have happened if you would have opened your mouth for once and told him how you feel?"

I laughed this time, laughed loud and long at the very idea. Of course my stupid subconscious was trying to make his relationship with Riley about me. Of course it was.

"It wouldn't matter. It wasn't like that with us."

"You'll never know now, will you?"

"What do you mean with us?" Jace asked, starting to get annoyed. "Who are you talking to?"

"You, or the ghost of you, I guess, who the fuck knows anymore. You're right. You knew I was in love with you. You teased me about it all the time like a sick piece of shit. But you weren't in love with me and I know that now. And honestly, asshole, I wasn't really even in love with you. Never again after that night. That was the point at which I was finally able to let you go. You just never paid attention enough to see it. Jesus-fucking-Christ."

I stopped talking and I knew I was dreaming because Jace had never been speechless once in his entire life. We sat in silence, for a few moments or a few years—it was all the same now.

"I couldn't have been in love with you. You know that."

The edge of the room was beginning to blur and the further I moved from the memory, the less clear everything became. Jace's dark jacket fell into tiny piles around him. My memories were turning into the ash that remained after a life is burned through. The last little embers of fire died and the room grew dark. I reached out to touch him and when I did, my hand pushed through him. Not like a ghost, but like a log after a slow burn. He dissolved, slowly between my fingers, coating them in a shadow of what used to be. And like that, he was gone.

When I opened my eyes, I felt a searing pain in my chest as I realized that every sleep would dilute my memories bit-by-bit until one day, it would be hard to remember what shade of blue Jace's eyes even were.

"Why didn't you tell him?" Dick asked in the dark.

"I already told you, it wouldn't have mattered."

"Maybe not to him, but it might have to you."

"Losing him never felt like an option," I said and realized how stupid that was as soon as the words left my mouth. It didn't really matter, after all. I tried everything I had and still lost him anyways. And yet, even after having lost him, I couldn't get rid of him. His pain was lodged in my heart and digging its way further and further into what was left of my soul, no matter how hard I tried.

"What time is it?"

"How should I know? I'm a duck."

I laughed before I could stop myself. "All these years and we never taught you how to tell time?"

"I couldn't wear a watch even if I wanted to." I heard the ruffle of feathers in the dark and felt a little wing inches from my nose. "I don't have a wrist, remember?"

"I know, Dick. I remember. Want to watch some TV?" I asked, climbing out of the bed.

"Sure. As long as it's not reruns of me. I can't stand watching myself on the screen. It's so cringe."

Yawning, I pulled one of my blankets off the bed and headed downstairs with my phone. It didn't really matter what time it was. I'd sit and watch the movement on the screen without seeing it and listen to the dialogue without hearing it until the sun came up and I could start it all over again.

I flipped through icon after icon on Netflix, but nothing sounded good.

"That one," Dick cried, pointing a little feather at the screen.

Surprised, I turned on the Quentin Tarantino movie I had stopped halfway through the week before and settled back. Dick stood on the couch and began acting out the scene, picking up right where I had left off, raising a gun and pointing it directly at me.

I woke up, alone on the couch, to the sound of my phone ringing. Daylight was starting to creep in past the curtains and the television was asking if I was still watching.

I looked at the name on the phone: *Barbara*

"What's up?" I asked as I answered.

"Listen, don't be mad," she started.

I had known Barbara for over seven years and felt like over that time had maybe lost my cool once or twice—total. Yet she always opened most of our conversations with, "don't be mad."

"What? Why would I be mad?"

"I was going to cancel with *Mercury* and forgot with every-thing going on and they called about it."

"Shit," I said, remembering countless conversations we had had about the interview with *Mercury* for weeks before Jace's death. It was supposed to be with both of us.

"I'm sorry I forgot."

"It's fine," I reassured. "Not a big deal. I should do it."

"No," she protested. "I'll push it."

"There's no sense in pushing it. At some point, we have to start doing normal things again and this is something we've been working on for a while. It is a little weird that it's all me now."

It hit me in that moment that anything related to promo-tions of *Dick* from that point on would be solely me. Jace was sporadic, flakey and often concerning, but he loved being in front of a camera. So much so, that one time in college I asked him why he was writing instead of acting and he told me with the straightest face he could manage that he was too ugly.

I could see now that he said that like he said everything, for shock and reassurance. He was a weak human who was terrified to show an ounce of vulnerability. But at the time, I remember being downright confused at how someone so beautiful could think that about himself. And if he thought that, what chance did I have.

"Johnny?" Barbara's voice on the other line pulled me from my daydreaming.

"Yeah," I answered. "I'm good. I'll do it. It's tomorrow, right?"

I had it in my calendar and knew it was there, but like everything in the past few weeks, I held it all at a safe distance.

"Yeah."

"Alright. I'll be there."

"Are you sure?"

I'd never been more sure of anything in my life.

"Yeah. Are we still doing dinner at Mark's Friday?"

"I think so. I haven't heard otherwise."

As soon as I was off the phone, I texted Annie to let her know I had personal things I had to deal with for the day and wouldn't be in the office, but I would be bringing by the journalist from *Mercury* tomorrow and to get the details from Barbara. I'm sure she breathed a sigh of relief at the sight. I wouldn't want me in her hair either. I only moved from the couch to go to the bathroom twice and get food once, but other than that, I remained horizontal the entire day. For a while, I watched Dick marching back and forth going upstairs and coming back down.

"What are you doing?" I asked finally.

"I'm pulling wardrobe for your interview tomorrow."

"No you're not. You can't even reach the clothes in my closet."

He stopped in his little tracks and ruffled his feathers aggressively, causing me to burst into laughter.

"Did you really just ruffle your feathers at me? Are you that miffed?"

"I'm trying to be useful."

"No you're not," I hedged. "You're trying to make me anxious. But it won't work. I'm going to sit here and watch shitty reality television and not think about the things I'll have to say tomorrow. Got it?"

He stomped away and I closed my eyes, listening to the soothing sounds of overproduced housewives yelling at one another over whether or not someone was doing drugs in the bathroom.

When I opened my eyes, I was standing outside of a diner, the first stop of the press tour. I was supposed to meet Roddy for breakfast and then take him around on my day. When Jace and I had the meeting about it, we had decided we were going to do breakfast at this diner, one of Jace's favorites, then a tour of the production offices before taking him shopping at the grocery store to prove what normal people we were, and finally dinner with a group that was going to look completely spontaneous and in no way staged.

"If we need to postpone this, we can," Roddy offered when he greeted me at the door.

"Nonsense," I said quickly and wondered if I had ever said the word 'nonsense' in my life. "I'm good. It's all good."

"I definitely don't want you to be uncomfortable."

I shook my head. "No, not at all. Let's get some food and talk about life."

We went inside and a waitress in a powder blue dress and

bright white apron approached us with a red painted smile and giant plastic menus. Jace loved anything that was a *thing* and the commitment of the diner to being *a thing* was, to some degree, impressive.

We sat down and took a minute of polite chit-chat to look at the menu before ordering. Without even being prompted, the waitress returned with two mugs of coffee.

"What made you pick this place?" he asked taking a drink of the stale coffee.

"Jace picked it," I admitted. "He loved this kind of thing."

"Why?"

"I don't know," I said. "The joke maybe? The cliché? Jace produced the reality he lived in and it was one that was built from Saturday cartoons and Quentin Tarantino films. He wanted to do slapstick bits while blood spattered the camera. It didn't have to make sense, if that makes sense."

In less time than it should have to make anything, she returned with two plates heaped full of breakfast foods.

"I'm going to ask questions about Jace, if that's okay?"

I looked down at my pancakes smiling back up at me. They didn't seem to give a shit, why should I?

"Let's do it."

"I want to jump right in, if that's okay."

"Of course," I said taking a bite.

"Your working partnership was well known around Hollywood. How did you two meet?"

"College. We had a screenwriting class together. The first week we had to pick critique partners and we sat next to one another, so in that sense, I guess it was fate based on where we sat that first day of class."

"And take me through the production company, and creation of *Dick* and all of that."

"Sure. We created *Dick* while in college, just as a side thing and then didn't really even pursue it until a few years down the road. We did a few short films and one of those really took off and got some attention. It was nominated for an Annie, which was such a big deal for us. But we both knew we wanted a show and we knew Dick was our best chance at that."

I was boring myself. There was a reason why Jace was always the person who did all the talking. *Jace the Face*, I always teased.

"Right on. But you had to fight sometimes, didn't you? How did you resolve that kind of conflict? I would guess it would be kind of like a marriage, right?"

"We rarely fought."

"That's a lie," Dick said in the booth next to me, blowing delicately over his steaming cup of coffee.

"Really?" Roddy asked, making a note in his notepad.

"I mean, yeah, sometimes, but not all the time, I would say."

"Lies," Dick jabbed.

"Jace was sometimes a difficult person to get along with, I guess," I cautiously admitted.

"Yeah?" Finally, some interest from the other side of the table.

"There was this one time..."

"Oh my god!" Dick interrupted, jumping up and down in the booth. "It's a mother-fucking clip show!"

"It's none of your business what the fuck it costs."

"It is when it's my literal fucking business, Jason."

"Ooh, Jason, you must be really mad if you're calling me Jason. Are you actually mad at me?" He crossed his arms and leaned against the kitchen counter under the bright florescent light.

He grinned like he enjoyed it. There were times I wondered if Jace thrived on conflict due to his chaotic childhood. There was no doubt to me that humor was the defense he learned early on to cope with his fear of abandonment. And when he wasn't getting his way, he set forth on a path of disruption to unbalance the world around him.

"I am mad; you're not taking this seriously. We are bleeding money at a rate we cannot sustain. If you want to keep this fucking show on the air, we're going to have to be smart about what we're spending. And when you go hire another fucking writer because you think she's hot, we have a goddamn problem, Jason." I emphasized his name this time.

"Are you jealous, Jonathan? Want me to hire a hot boy for you to look at?"

"Fuck you," I exhaled, moving around the kitchen island toward the fridge. "You're such a fucking dick sometimes. I'm so fucking sick of feeling sorry for you."

Before I knew it, a glass smashed into the cabinet next to me.

"What the fuck?!" I screamed, shifting away from the counter. "What the actual fuck?"

"I'm sorry," he said, raising his hands quickly. "I'm so sorry. I didn't mean to do that."

I stared at him and didn't know if I could even believe him anymore.

He moved quickly around to grab a broom and dustpan and began sweeping up the glass in silence. I watched him bent over, focused solely on the glass and a look on his face like he was about to cry. My anger dissolved at the sight of his glistening eyes. After he was finished, he dumped it in the trash and moved close to me. I debated whether or not I should scoot away from him. I had a feeling he was going to try to touch me.

"You're right. It was stupid and I'm a dick. I'm sorry. I promise I won't do it again."

"I don't want to fight with you," I said gently, running both hands through my hair, "but sometimes you have to listen to what I'm saying. Especially when it's about numbers. You know you're not a numbers guy."

"I know. I know this. You're the only person who will ever tell me the truth about this kind of shit. I'm so sorry."

He reached out like he was going to touch my shoulder but stopped himself.

"It's fine. But I need to fire one of them. It can either be Annie or you'll have to pick someone else. We can't afford all of them."

"Fire Evan. He's an asshole. Annie's staying."

"Evan really is an asshole," I agreed.

Jace laughed quietly and sniffed as he leaned against the counter next to me, moving close enough to push his shoulder into mine. And just like that, it was over.

———

"And then they kissed," Dick offered.

We didn't. He knew that.

"I think that might have been one of the worst fights we ever had."

"Over whether or not Dick wore a fedora?" Roddy laughed. "That's pretty funny. Sounds like you guys had good communication then."

"Yeah, I would say so," I lied.

"And you won, obviously."

"I think Jace let me win. Sometimes he would let me win."

"He had kind of a reputation—you must have known—for being kind of abrasive and a little unpredictable."

"Really?" I asked, sounding as surprised as I could. "I guess I didn't know."

Roddy smiled like he knew I was laying it on a little too thick at this point.

"I need to know, and this can be off the record if you want... did he really get kicked out of Elton John's Oscar's party?"

"No," I said, "on the record, that's a rumor. I've heard that before. I do know he got kicked out of quite a few other places. In college, for instance—"

<hr>

"You've got to shut the fuck up," Jace said, grabbing my elbow as I tried to walk away.

"Who is going to stop me?" I challenged.

"I will, you stupid mother fucker. We're going to get kicked out. We're not even supposed to be here."

The music was blaring so loud all I could make out was the deep bass beats rattling my ribs with every second.

"He was calling you a little bitch."

"I do not care, John, he's an idiot," he yelled over the music.

"Why are you so calm about this?" I slurred. "You're the hothead of the group."

He laughed. "Because I'm nowhere near as drunk as you, moron. You've got to stop. I'm asking you to stop."

"He called your work reductive."

Jace laughed even louder at this. "It is! Everything is reductive. All work everywhere is reductive, except fucking Shakespeare. You're wasted. Let's go home."

"Okay," I wiggled out of his grip and we began walking toward the door.

I wasn't wasted. I was drunk, but I wasn't wasted. Could a wasted person wave goodbye to Katy Perry? No, they couldn't. A wasted person couldn't have even stood up straight, let alone waved to the queen.

"Just stay here for a minute," he said, planting me in one place as he moved to speak to someone I didn't know. She was really pretty though.

Everyone Jace talked to was always really pretty. He didn't waste his time if they weren't. He had a type, for sure.

"You're still here?" Howard asked, moving closer. "Tell me, who did Jace fuck to get in? I'm dying to know."

"Okay," I said, waving my hand in his face. "You can fuck off."

"It had to be good. He must have a magical little dick. I bet you know all about that."

Before I could stop myself, I shoved against his shoulder. "Is that reductive, bitch?"

Howard pulled back to punch me. I knew the alcohol had given me courage, but I had no idea it had also given me superpowers, and I was able to move backwards as the punch tried to land, only barely grazing my chin.

"Holy shit," I heard Jace yell behind me when he saw what was going on.

He rushed over to grab me as I staggered back and pulled my waist toward the door, looking at my face in the process. "Are you okay? I told you to stand still. Fuck off, Howard!"

I stumbled in his arms as we rushed to the door. "We gotta go."

"What the fuck is wrong with you?" he cackled.

We exited into the crisp night air and his laughter echoed around us as we took off, running down the sidewalk as confused onlookers watched us stagger into the darkness.

———

"And then they kissed," Dick said with a sigh, resting his wings gently under his chin.

We definitely didn't.

"But he always found a way to get out of the situations he got himself into. Most kids would have gotten expelled for that kind of stunt, but he talked his way out of it. He always did."

Roddy laughed. "Wild. He sounded wild."

"He was. He softened quite a bit as we got older, I think. Mellowed a little. I can't imagine what he would have been like as an old man. Guess we'll never know."

Roddy sobered a little and took a drink of his water. "I'm sorry, I didn't mean to make it all about this."

"No," I said, leaning back. "It's actually kind of nice. Thinking back on all our good times together."

"Let's switch gears. You're an openly gay writer. Can we talk a little bit about the responsibility you have to produce gay stories?"

"I don't really talk about that."

"Why is that? There aren't any queer characters in *Dick*, are there?"

"How many times do people ask you if you're straight? How often do people ask you if your work promotes your own identity? Is your identity always reduced to who you're sleeping with?"

"Just seems like you could do a lot to help your community by promoting those kinds of stories. The under-represented have the opportunity to make things better for those to come."

I sighed and looked down at my pancakes. The mouth had melted and dripped over the edge.

"Am I making you uncomfortable? Would you like to talk about something else?"

"Yes, please."

"Let's focus on *Dick*."

"Finally," he grumbled next to me.

"Where do you see it going from here? Now?"

"We're still going strong," I said, taking a drink of coffee. "Jace's passing won't change that."

"What did it feel like, the first time you saw an episode on television?"

"It was unreal. We had a little watch party that night."

———

I held the theater door open as Jace walked past me into the lobby.

"I don't even know what to say. I have no words right now."

I laughed. "Me either. So much sadder than I thought it would be. Talk about kill your gays."

"Yeah. For real. Let's never waste our time on anything other than comedy. Please."

He had gotten a few steps ahead of me and held the door as we walked out into the parking lot. There were puddles around us from a rare L.A. rain that had passed through while we were inside. Jace stopped to zip up his jacket.

"Like, why?"

I shook my head.

"Sometimes I wish I could find out what is going on in those pitch meetings where something like that gets greenlit. I know we could write something better than that if we ever got the chance." As he said this, he pulled his cigarettes out of his pocket and lit one.

"Just unnecessarily sad."

He started to walk a few steps but stopped, turning to me, cigarette in hand. "Can I ask you something?"

"Sure."

"Did your parents react badly at all when you came out to them?"

"Oh," I said. "Badly? I wouldn't say badly. I think

surprised, maybe, a little? My parents have always been supportive, I think. Sometimes they just don't know how, maybe. Why?"

"Gay movies always make it this teary-eyed sweet thing. But it's probably not, always. Right?" He offered me the cigarette and I took a long drag on it.

"I would guess so," I said, unsure if I could speak to every gay experience. "I do think movies romanticize it, if that makes sense. But those movies are probably made by straight people. For sure that movie was made by a straight person."

He smiled and started walking again. "Does it bother you?"

"That straight people make gay movies?"

He nodded.

"Not really. I make straight movies."

His laugh echoed in the air around us and I listened to the splash of his shoe making contact with one of the puddles.

"Would you rather make gay movies? Like, is that important to you?"

"I just want to make anything." I left out the, with you, that rested in my brain. It wasn't the content that mattered to me. It was the chance to do it with him. He took the cigarette from my lips and took a drag.

"I think sometimes I don't think about that, like how it's different for you, sometimes. So, I guess, what I mean, is if you wanted to promote that, I'd be down to, you know?"

"Yeah," I nodded. "Thanks, man."

"Whatever is important to you is important to me. You know that, right?"

"Of course. And the same with you."

"I do love you, you know? Like, not gay I mean, but like you're my best friend. And I love you. I can say that, right? That's not weird?"

I laughed as I watched him pull the cigarette stub out and

toss it to the ground. "Yeah, you can say that and yeah, you're being weird. But I know that. I love you too."

And then we did kiss.

———

"I knew it!" Dick yelled, jumping up on the table to point down at me from the high ground like Tom Cruise on Oprah's couch.

Jace did kiss me. But not like that. Not in a romantic way. That night in the parking lot, Jace and I hugged and he landed a big smooch on my cheek before he got in his car and drove away.

"That's sweet," Roddy commented, making notes, "and very creative with the little rubber ducks as decorations."

"Yeah, we went through a phase early on where everything we did was all about little ducks. In fact," I reached into my pocket and pulled out a tiny glass duck we would carry around for promotion, "you can have this one. We had so many made, I still have a few boxes in my house."

Roddy held it up and Dick shuffled closer to inspect it, as though making sure it was up to his avian standards.

"If you're ready, we can take a trip to the production offices and you can meet some folks there? I can drive us."

"That sounds great."

I got the bill and paid for it while he took a minute to go to the restroom. "You're driving?" Dick asked. "Is that a good idea?"

I noticed a teenage girl staring from across the room and I pulled out my phone to let Annie know we were going to stop by.

"You think it's a bad idea?"

"Can I get a picture?" I heard from the other side of my phone.

"Of me?" I asked, confused.

She nodded and I wanted to tell her I wasn't whatever actor she was imagining in case she heard any of the interview and thought I was someone she needed a picture with.

"I'm Jonathan Goodwin."

"I can't believe I saw you here. I'm a big fan."

"Of me?" I asked again, still confused.

"Yeah. *Midnight Dolly* is one of my favorite movies of all time."

"Oh, thank you," I said, surprised. "Well, yeah, let's get a picture."

I posed and she leaned in front of me to snap the photo on her cell phone.

"Here," I said quickly, pulling one of the extra little ducks from my pocket. "Take a duck."

Her face lit up as she accepted it but then grew somber quickly. "Thank you. I'm really sorry about Jace."

"Yeah," I agreed. "Me too."

Roddy appeared behind her and watched the exchange. When she hurried away, he moved closer. "Did you pay her to do that?"

"I wish I was smart enough to even think of that."

We walked outside into the pleasant morning air. I directed him to my blue Prius.

"This is me," I said.

We got in the car and he pulled out his phone to start texting as I turned on the engine, and my jazz station started playing.

"There's no need to be nervous or anything," I joked before promptly backing into a car.

"Oh my god!" he cried, gripping the dashboard after the crunch of the bumper ended.

"No, it's fine," I reassured, turning off the car and getting out to look at the damage.

"There's damage. You hit the fucking car."

"Yeah," I agreed. I had.

I began to wonder if he would write a story about how he nearly died in the car at the hands of Jonathan Goodwin. That couldn't be good for my brand.

He said nothing but looked at me over the trunk of the car as though scared of what was coming next. I wondered what Jace would have done.

"Okay, hold on, it's fine." I made my way back into the car to find something to write on. "I'll leave a note."

His face held a hint of skepticism. "Should we call the cops?"

"Nonsense," I said for the second time that day, with as much confidence as I could possibly muster. "I think it's okay. It's an insurance thing."

"You don't even know how to drive a car?" Dick said, pointing at the bumper. "God, what a fucking idiot."

"Alright," I muttered, moving toward the other vehicle. "See? I'll just leave a note. It will be fine. It's fine."

Roddy looked at me like he thought maybe it wasn't fine. Jace would have been beside himself in laughter had he been present. Of course, I reasoned, if he was alive, he would be the one driving, not me.

"We're good—we're good," I said as I carefully tucked the handwritten note under the windshield of the other car. "Ready?"

I turned up my jazz a little to fill the awkward silence of the car. Dick was in the back seat, buckled up safe and sound.

"So, what else do you want to talk about?" I asked as I pulled out into the road, determined to drive safer than I had in my entire life.

"Do you feel like you want to keep making *Dick* without Jace? This isn't for the interview, I think this is my own personal curiosity."

"Oh," I said, watching a car zoom up on my right-hand side. "I do. It's more than me and Jace, you know? It's my own personal investment of years of work. And realistically the show is set up to operate without me or Jace being involved; it's not like we're the only people who make it happen. We've got a team of really fantastic writers, producers, actors—all of that is a giant group effort."

"Right. Diplomatic answer."

I said nothing as we turned.

"Can we shift gears to talk about you? What was your childhood like?"

"Uh," I started, "you know, little gay film kid growing up in rural Texas? It practically writes itself."

Roddy laughed. "That bad?"

"Not bad, I guess. A little cliché."

"Do you have siblings?"

"A brother. We aren't close."

I didn't elaborate and he didn't seem like he was interested in pushing it, despite it being the exact reason he was here.

"Jesus Christ, you're bad at this," Dick quacked. "Aren't you boring yourself? How do you expect him to write an article about a brother you refuse to even talk about?"

"Sorry," I said after a beat of silence. "I was nervous about doing this by myself and Jace was really the one in front of the camera most of the time. I'm trying to get used to being that guy now. It's still kind of weird for me. So, sorry."

"You don't have to apologize," Roddy said, and it felt like he meant it. "I lost my dad three years ago to suicide. It fucks you up."

My whole body exhaled. "Yeah, it really does. I'm sorry to hear that. How did you handle it?"

"You're supposed to be doing the interview, dipshit!" Dick yelled from the backseat.

"I'm still in therapy. I don't know that some of that ever goes away," Roddy offered.

"Is this relevant?!"

"I'm really struggling," I admitted.

"Honestly? I blacked out a lot of it. Like it all kind of seems like one big blur now," he said, turning toward me slightly in the passenger seat.

Without turning to look, I kept nodding and didn't know what else to say.

I turned the car one final time as we pulled into the production parking lot. Relieved that we both made it one piece, I turned off the car.

"Can I be honest with you, Johnny?"

"Sure."

"I requested this story once I found out what happened with Jace. It wasn't supposed to be me writing it. But I went to our editor and asked if I could do it. There's this weird kind of understanding you get when you meet someone else who has gone through a loss like that. It can be so isolating, but I guess I wanted you to know you're not the only one, you know?"

I stared at the steering wheel as though expecting it to offer some kind of wisdom. I wanted it to bond us, certainly, but I had this dread in my stomach when I realized that I didn't feel any more connected to him, because I didn't feel anything. The numbness that had settled in my life since Jace died was stronger than ever.

"Thanks, man," I said instead. "That's really helpful to hear."

He smiled and I was so desperately jealous of his ability to have survived the death around him. In that moment, I worried that I would never be able to move past it. That I would forever be stuck in this half-dead realm with a Jace-sized hole in my heart.

"Want to see the offices?" I asked with a cheerful grin.

"Let's do it."

He got out of the car and Dick got out of the car and I worried I wouldn't, or couldn't. What if I maybe stayed in the car forever? Rotting away until I finally closed my eyes for the last time. Unable to move.

Stuck.

Here.

Alone.

"You coming?"

"Yep," I said, pulling out the keys and opening the door.

I put one foot in front of the other and smiled at Annie at the door, opened wide in anticipation, ready to give the grand tour. Annie and Roddy shook hands and she started in with bright eyes and earnest smiles.

Life continued on without me present. Jace was right, I didn't need to be there at all.

As Roddy pushed into the office door, Annie looked at me with nothing but concern.

"Are you okay?"

"We got into a wreck, but it's okay," I said quickly, holding the door open as she walked through it.

"What?" she gasped quietly.

"We're good. All alive."

"Why don't you take a moment? I'll give him a tour and give you about twenty minutes?"

"You're the best," I said, grabbing her shoulder before she

moved back to where Roddy was waiting. Jace was right about that too. Hiring her had been one of the best decisions he had made. She was a godsend.

"What can we do with twenty minutes?" Dick asked at my feet.

"I'm closing my eyes and seeing if you disappear in the process," I said as I started in the direction of my office.

"Dick," I heard him mumble behind me as he waddled quickly in my wake.

SEASON 1 - EPISODE 4
The Bottle Episode

I pulled up to Mark's house and turned off the car, psyching myself up to do what needed to be done. I thought about canceling, but I knew Riley was going and it would be nice to see her. Plus, I hadn't sat at a table for a real meal in over a week, so I could pull it together enough to be social for a few hours. Seeing Jace's car sitting in the driveway hit me in a place I hadn't expected.

Grabbing my bottle of wine, I headed up the driveway to the front door, waiting for Dick to follow. He was mid-sentence as he rushed over and stood at the door, smoothing his hair like he was nervous.

"Are you wearing a tuxedo?" I started to ask, but cut myself off when the door opened.

Mark stood there, arms out. I moved forward to give him a hug and hand over my bottle.

"Johnny!" Toni said from behind him. "I'm so glad you made it."

Toni was nearly twenty years younger than Mark and played the part of Hollywood housewife to a tee. I tugged at my suit jacket and shuffled forward to give her a hug.

"What are you drinking? Wine? Beer? Liquor?"

"Wine would be great. White."

She disappeared toward the kitchen and Mark waved us into the living room. "Gang's all here."

"Great, thanks."

I walked along the polished floor into one of the grand living rooms that looked like no one lived in it. My footsteps echoed on the marble tiles as I moved and I wondered why I was so self-conscious of it. Along with my steps, I could hear the little padded gait of Dick as he rushed alongside me to keep up with my long legs.

Riley stood up from her seat and headed directly to me.

"You look nice," I said as she approached.

"Thanks," she said with a smile. "You know this is the first time in weeks that I've put on makeup? It was kind of nice, having a reason to."

"Me too," I said, and she laughed before catching herself.

The familiar sadness filled her eyes and it hurt me inside to visibly see the life draining from her eyes as she remembered why laughing felt weird these days. It made me want to hate Jace that he had hurt her in this way.

"I heard about Blake," she said after a few moments. "I'm really sorry."

"Oh, I know you don't mean that. I'm not, really, when it comes down to it."

"Good. He was so bad for you."

I smiled as Mark walked up with a glass of wine and offered it in my direction.

"Thank you," I said, taking the alcohol from him.

"What are we talking about?"

"My recent ex-boyfriend," I said before taking a drink.

"Oh? You know, if you're interested, I know a few single men who are ready to mingle. Whenever you are."

Riley covered her mouth with her glass. I tried to imagine the kind of man Mark had in mind. Despite his open proclamations of progressivism and multiple fundraisers for Barack Obama, I wasn't quite sure if he actually knew many gay people other than myself. In fact, I wondered if I was usually the one he used when he told stories and wanted to include *his Gay Friend* and if Riley was *his Black Friend*.

"That's kind of you. I'd be open. I'm already ready to get back in the dating pool, I think. Realistically, Blake and I were broken up long before it was official."

Riley raised an eyebrow at this, but said nothing. I wanted to add that really it was because most of my days now were spent alone and I was beginning to fear the idea of getting older by myself forever, but figured that wasn't the kind of thing you say at a dinner party that's already awkward enough with the ghost of your mutual friend.

The truth was that being alone had never really crossed my mind before, because I knew I wouldn't be. Jace and I were going to be around each other for decades and decades. We had talked ad nauseam about retiring together on a beach somewhere. With Riley, of course, but it would always be us together. And I think in my mind, I had some ambiguous partner there, sharing my life, but the anchor of it all was always Jace when I thought about it.

"Jonathan Goodwin!" Barbara yelled from across the room. "Why did you try to kill that nice journalist?"

"Hold on," I protested, raising my glass. "I didn't *try* to kill him."

"What?" Riley asked, confused.

"I might have had a little fender bender in the parking lot of Dilly's."

"What?" Mark jumped in.

"It wasn't *that* bad."

"He said his life flashed before his eyes."

"Okay, he's being dramatic," I pleaded. "Do you think that will influence the story at all?"

"You better hope not. That's nothing more than what you need."

I shrugged.

"When will you see the article?" Barbara's boyfriend asked.

I recognized him, but could not for the life of me remember his name. He and Barbara had been dating for a while and she always complained about him to us with the moniker 'The Boy' as though he didn't have a name, or maybe she never remembered it either.

"I don't know," I replied honestly. "They'll probably send it to Barbara first."

The Boy looked to her and smiled as though that was a thing to be proud of.

"You better hope now it doesn't make you look bad."

"Well, I think half of it will be about Jace and no one can hate on that."

The others grew quiet, but I noticed Riley laughing silently.

"What's funny about that?" I asked.

"Can you imagine," she said through little gasps, "what Jace would have done if he had been there? He'd never let you live that down."

I smiled, knowing she was right. "God, he would have been insufferable."

The others joined in the laughter and I wondered if that would be how it was when I died—if people would stand around rooms and tell stories about that one time I did something stupid and everyone would laugh.

We all got quiet again and I could feel the tension in every muscle. Would it be like this all night, with awkward pauses when we all stopped to honor Jace's memory?

One of the catering staff moved around the room offering little hors d'oeuvres. I declined politely as Riley took one of the little crackers. The Boy was clearly trying to come up with something to say.

"When do the Emmy nominations come out?" he blurted.

I looked to Mark.

"Should be soon."

"Have you heard anything?" I asked.

He shook his head.

"Do you have to be invited? To the ceremony?"

They all started in on a general discussion that inevitably steered toward the last time we had all gone to the ceremony together. I barely heard anything that was said.

"Excuse me," I offered, moving away to the restroom.

I pulled my pants down and sat on the toilet. When I looked up Dick was standing directly in front of me, watching closely.

"Jesus!" I yelled, startled by his sudden appearance.

He laughed and I imagined a scenario in which he pulled out a giant knife like Chucky and killed me.

"I'm not going to kill you," he said languidly. "How dare you insult me by comparing me to Chucky."

"I wasn't, I mean—"

I stopped arguing with myself and focused on taking a shit.

"Oh, you're not going to talk to me any more?" Dick asked, crossing his wings.

"Why bother? I'm you, remember?"

"Good point. This party is so boring. You should do something to liven it up. What would Jace do?"

"Jace would be drunk," I said as I flushed the toilet and turned on the faucet.

"Then you need to drink up, it sounds like. We've been stuck in this house for hours now. Wait," he said as though struck with an idea, "is this a bottle episode?"

"It's not an episode, this isn't television, not everything is a trope. It's a fucking dinner party and you're not real remember?"

"That really hurts, Johnny," he cried, pretending to wipe away tears from his shiny little eyes.

"Alright. That's enough. And if it was a bottle episode, it'd be a fucking boring one. Also, it hasn't been hours. It's been like forty minutes tops."

"Oh my god. You could drop something dramatic on them. Why not confess your love for Jace? Or Riley? That'd really be a hoot."

"Okay, stop."

"What if you killed Mark?"

"Jesus Christ. What the fuck is wrong with you?"

"I'm bored!" Dick yelled, jumping up and flapping his way up to the sink.

"I've never really thought about how you can fly," I said, distracted.

"What?"

"You can fly. You can actually fly."

"Of course I can fly, I'm a duck."

I rubbed my hand against the towel before reaching for the

door. "So that's it? You're here now? You'll be here the whole time?"

"It's *my* show," he said indignantly.

"This isn't a show," I grumbled as I opened the door.

"Then who are they?" Dick asked, pointing to the audience.

I followed his wing, before leaving. I returned into the living room and watched as Dick went from person to person, pulling out a giant butcher knife and eyeing me wildly as he acted like he was going to stab each of them. What the fuck was wrong with me?

When he got to The Boy, The Boy looked right where Dick was holding the knife and a chill ran down my spine. Was it possible The Boy had the ability to see Dick? Why would that be? Was he more important than I had originally thought to our plot?

The moment passed as he leaned forward to get another piece of food from the tray.

"He's not important," Dick cried, turning around and waddling back in my direction. "You don't even know his name. If he was important, he would have a name."

He has a name, I wanted to say, but didn't. I didn't know his name.

"Bob? Timothy? Francis? Macaroni? Cliff? Biff? Boff?"

I glared at Dick who was getting louder with each guess.

"Are you okay?" Riley asked, looking at my face with concern.

"Yeah," I said, taking another drink.

"Dinner is almost ready!" Toni announced. "Let's take our seats."

I looked at Toni and her sympathetic eyes. Toni intercepted me and took my wine glass out of my hand. "Let me refresh your drink."

"Oh, thanks," I offered.

She winked at me and I tried to control my eyebrows as she disappeared.

We sat around the giant walnut table, over-adorned with runners, candles, flowers and everything else Toni could think to add. Riley was on my right and she offered a quick smile as we sat.

As soon as Toni returned with my glass and the others had been served fresh drinks, Mark stood.

"A toast," he said, raising his glass. "We honor the memory of our dear friend, Jason. Not a day goes by that we don't miss his sense of humor and infectious laugh. I know the office will never be the same without hearing his laugh from across the room."

It was true. I missed his laugh a lot. It was the loud kind of laugh that always felt genuine. As though every joke he heard was the first one in the world, and he was the first person to hear it.

The night before, I had played a video on my phone over and over to hear his laugh again. It was becoming harder to recall it in my mind and I knew that eventually it would be nothing more than a fuzzy memory like the rest of him.

Riley held up her glass next to me and I looked over in her direction, noticing for the first time that she wasn't wearing her wedding ring. I had never seen her without it since their wedding.

"He had the best laugh," Barbara agreed.

"Here, here," The Boy joined.

We all paused to touch glasses before taking a drink.

"Do you want to say anything?" Mark asked.

We all looked to him and realized he was asking Riley. Her eyes widened but she stood.

"Thank you all for your support and love during these last

few weeks. I wish I had a better explanation of what brought us here. I wish we could go back and do so many things differently. But we can't. We're given the life that we're given and I'm grateful that each and every one of you here is in my life. I'm also grateful I got to spend the time I did with Jace in my life. I know you all miss him as much as I do every day."

We all cheered and raised our glasses again as Riley sat down. Toni stood and offered a Hollywood salute—hands clasped together, shaking gently—before she headed back into the kitchen. In a matter of moments, the chef entered with plates and a few uniformed workers began putting food in front of us.

General chatter resumed and I leaned toward Riley. "That was really lovely."

"Thanks. I'd love to talk about literally anything else."

I tried to think about anything that didn't involve Jace, Dick or death and had absolutely nothing.

The plate held delicately portioned foams and sauces smeared across the ceramic. I picked up my fork and reached for the vegetables on the far side of the plate.

Mark had started in on the reality of what climate change meant for changing shorelines in L.A. and I didn't even care. I knew it was real and scary but like everything else lately, it didn't even matter. So what if the whole city found itself underwater in the next decade? What the fuck was I supposed to do about it? The ocean was going to consume us all eventually; that was truly inevitable.

"What are we going to do about the voice?" I asked.

A silence fell around the table.

"What?" Mark asked, looking at me.

"Dick has Jace's voice. What are you going to do about the voice?"

"Oh, well, we'll need to figure that out."

I knew they already had. They had likely made the decision within days of Jace's death. They would recast—I knew that—but for some reason I wanted him to say it to my face.

"What do you think we should do?" Mark asked after a moment.

"I don't know. I mean, we don't have access to Jace's voice anymore."

Riley shifted next to me.

"Maybe we circle back to this?" Barbara replied.

"I think it would make me feel better if I knew. You know, in Jace's memory."

I felt a nudge against my leg and realized it was Riley.

"Johnny," Barbara said, more stern this time. "Let's drop it. Please."

It didn't really strike me as something that was particularly hurtful or rude. I thought it was important to be discussed with the exact people sitting in the room. Mark would do whatever cost him the least. And Barbara didn't even have a dog in the fight anymore.

"Sure," I said finally. "It doesn't really matter, I guess."

Circle back. We can circle back on the decision to find a human that will mimic the noises of our dead friend. Sure, let's circle back.

I looked at Toni and she had a sympathetic look on her face. "Can I get you another glass of wine?"

"Now you've done it!" Dick yelled, laughing from the corner where he sat on top of a decorative table, using the giant black Tom Ford coffee table book as his personal dinner tray. "Good choice. That was about as dramatic as I've ever seen you be! And about me, no less. Good form, Johnny. Good form."

"I've got it," I offered, as I stood. As soon as I opened the door I noticed Toni coming up behind me.

"How are you doing? Really?" she asked.

"I'm good."

She moved closer and I backed up into the cabinet. "I can't stop thinking about how sad you must be. And lonely."

"Yeah."

Suddenly her hand was over mine and she squeezed it. "I'm here for you, Jonathan."

"Thanks?" I offered, hoping it didn't come out as much of a question as I felt.

"Anything you need, you just let me know. Anything at all."

I wondered how upset she would be if I let her know the thing I needed was for her to back up a few inches.

"More wine?" I said, raising the glass between us.

She laughed and moved away to get the bottle. "Always with the jokes. You and Jace were always full of jokes."

"That's why they paid us the big bucks."

She laughed again as she began to pour.

"Thank you," I said, raising the glass once she stopped.

The bottle clinked loudly as it made contact with the granite countertops and Toni moved closer again to grab my shoulder. "I'm glad you're here."

"Thank you for inviting me."

I inched away and smiled as I backed out and headed back into the dining room. Riley's eyes flicked over and one of her eyebrows arched in question as I sat.

I shook my head slightly and she turned to look at Toni entering the room. I kept my eyes down at my plate while she tried to hide a smile.

It felt like I stared at the food in front of me until everyone was scooting back, preparing to leave. Quickly, I gave Mark and Toni hugs before wishing everyone a goodbye.

I moved to the door, preparing to say goodbye to Riley.

"Can I ask you a favor?" she asked before I had a chance to say goodnight.

"Yeah," I responded, patting my pant legs, looking for my keys. "Anything you need, you know that."

"Can you—" she started, stopping a minute as she found her resolve, "Can you come over tonight? So I can sleep?"

"Oh." Her request surprised me. "Yes, of course."

"I haven't slept a good night's sleep since, you know. I close my eyes and all I see is what was left of his face. Staring back at me. I can't make it stop..."

"Oh my god, Riley, why didn't you ask sooner?" I asked, putting my hands on her shoulders.

"It now only seems silly," she said quietly. "I was fine when my mom was here and I think I thought it was fine and everything, but once she left, I kind of stopped? And now it's really hit and miss. I'm so exhausted, I need like one good night's sleep."

"I'd be honored to sleep with you," I teased, pulling her close and was glad she laughed in my embrace. "What time?"

She checked her phone. "Does 11:00 pm work?"

"Yes. I'll be there."

I said my goodbyes to everyone, and Riley and I walked out at the same time. I paused near my car as I watched her make her way to Jace's before getting inside. My eyes fell on my crumpled bumper before I opened the car door.

"Jesus," Dick declared, moving a little closer to look at the damage. "You're such a wreck. Literally."

"Alright."

Once eleven rolled around, my car practically drove itself to Jace's house. It was a route I could have made with my eyes closed. When I pulled up, I felt the familiar stab in my chest that had lodged itself there. I grabbed my phone and saw the text from Riley. *Door's open.*

Pushing against the heavy front door, I looked around the empty house that even felt different now. I hadn't been over since the funeral. Prior to Jace's diminishment, I was over almost every day. Once he was gone, I had... ceased. It felt weird, now, like being here was somehow intruding. It was no longer our space, it was Riley's and I was an outsider.

I was conscious of how every object around the room was now a symbol of Jace's life. When he was alive and we were in this room spit-balling ideas for season finales of *Dick*, it was a lamp. Now, it was one of the few pieces of furniture he had carried from his disgusting college dorm into his Hollywood Hills home. An artifact of Jace's origin story. A prop.

She had removed a lot of the things that belonged to him and I couldn't really blame her. The space was hers now after all. She was leaning against the doorframe between the front room and the kitchen.

"Weird, isn't it?"

I nodded.

"Like you know he's not here. And never will be again. How does that happen?" she asked.

"I don't know."

"I think I kind of thought I would expect him, you know? Like I'd be waiting for him to come home or hear something inside and think it's him. But I don't. It's so final."

"Can I?" I asked, pointing toward the garage.

She visibly shivered. "Knock yourself out. I can't anymore. I'm going upstairs to change."

After she moved away, I headed to the door through the kitchen and braced myself before turning the little brass knob. The room was cold and my brain instantly went to the *Sixth Sense* before I could stop it.

"Wow, this is where the magic happened?" Dick's voice echoed, causing me to physically jump.

"Jesus," I hissed. "You scared the shit out of me."

He waddled past me, moving right to the spot where Jace's body was when I arrived that day. Riley had covered him with a tarp and I was glad I hadn't seen his mangled flesh before he was carted out. Where the body was, a darkened patch of what I guessed was his leftover blood remained. A piece of him that would never go away.

Without knowing why, I bent over and put my hand on the concrete, letting the cold spread across my fingers.

"What the fuck are you doing?" Dick asked, shuffling up to me.

"I don't know."

"Are you trying to absorb his old blood? Osmosis the shit out of a dead man?"

"You can't tell time but you know osmosis?" I asked sarcastically.

He shrugged as he plopped down on the ground. "Kind of freaky."

"Yeah, it is kind of freaky," I agreed.

I didn't know what I wanted or expected. There was nothing here—no lingering traces of Jace's ghost or soul. The only piece of him was a figment of my broken mind. Well, and his bleached-out blood.

"Pathetic," Jace mumbled, and I didn't know if it was directed at me or what was left of him.

"Come on," I said, standing back up. "Let's get back inside."

When I closed the door, Riley was leaning against the counter in the kitchen.

"I can't even go in there," she said, pushing back and forth on the stone countertop.

"I'm sorry."

"And I can't afford to buy something else—so I'm stuck here for now."

"You could move in with me?" I offered without thinking.

She smiled, but it was sad. "No, I love this house and this area. I'm bummed that I can never use the garage again. Such a dick for that."

"He *would* ruin a perfectly good garage."

"And the shirt he was wearing? Destroyed."

"Not to mention the tarp. You had to throw that away."

She pointed to me in agreement. "You're right. What a fucking asshole."

"It was probably at least twelve to fifteen dollars."

"At least."

We stood in silence and I stared at my feet, unsure of what else there was to say. "I'm so tired," she said after a minute. "Are you ready to go to bed?"

"Sure."

Carefully, I followed her upstairs and into the bedroom. She moved away into the bathroom. "I'll be a minute."

"Sure."

I walked into the room and stood awkwardly by the desk that was up against the large window. I could only think of a handful of times I had been in Jace's bedroom and one of them was only because the downstairs toilet was broken.

It looked like a mixture of Jace and Riley, and somehow, still happy. My eyes fell on a pile of Jace's clothes on a chair. I moved closer and picked up a dark button up shirt, smelling it to get a hint of him back in my brain. It smelled like Old Spice and stale cigarette smoke and my memory activated so quickly I felt like someone was squeezing my insides. I let it fall back on top of the pile.

"Do you want any of his clothes?" she asked behind me. "I'm going to get rid of all of those."

"No," I said, running my hand over the fabric one more time. "His stuff wouldn't fit me anyways."

I was slightly taller than Jace with longer arms, and the few times we had tried to swap clothes his sleeves never were long enough. I turned around to face Riley. She was adjusting the top of the bonnet on her head and I watched her ritual carefully.

"What, have you never seen a Black girl get ready for bed?" she asked.

"Riley," I started, pushing one shoe off with the other, "in what context would I have seen *any* girl getting ready for bed?"

She laughed loudly as she pulled the top blanket back. "Fair enough. I'm sorry if this is weird."

"It's not weird. I would want Jace to keep my fictitious gay husband company if the roles were reversed."

She laughed again as she climbed into the bed. "Okay. I'm sorry, but it looks insane with you standing over there watching me. Can you sit in the bed, at least for a little bit, until I fall asleep?"

"Sure."

I pulled my shoes over to the side of the chair before getting into bed on the side that I knew must have been Jace's. It did feel a little weird, but I didn't want to make Riley feel bad. If this is what she needed to get some sleep, I was willing to be as weird as possible.

She reached around and turned off the lamp, sending us into a shroud of darkness.

"Thank you, Johnny," she said, and I could hear the tiredness in her voice. "I don't know how to sleep in a bed by myself anymore."

I reached over and wrapped my arm around hers in the dark. "I'm so sorry."

"It's okay," she whispered. "You know he knew."

"Knew what?"

"How much you loved him."

"Yeah," I said. "I know."

We sat there, in pitch black nothingness, holding each other, hoping that the other could eventually find their way out of the dark room we were both stuck in. I guessed in this way it was up to us to help each other, but I didn't even know how. Half of the time when I opened my mouth, I felt like I was making things worse.

When I woke up, there was light coming through the tops of the curtains. Riley was turned away, but curled up right against my body. It was the best sleep I had gotten since Jace died that didn't involve Nyquil or straight liquor.

I didn't know how long I laid there, staring up at the ceiling before Riley moved next to me.

"Thank you," she said, rubbing her fingers over her eyes. "I needed that so much. I fell asleep instantly."

"I do tend to have that effect on people."

"Want some breakfast?" she asked as she rolled out of bed and headed to the bathroom.

"Sure."

"Question," she said when she walked back in. "Was Toni hitting on you last night or was that part of my dream?"

"Okay," I said, turning toward her in the bed. "I really thought so, but she knows I'm gay, so I didn't know. But that was weird, right?"

"Very weird," Riley said with a laugh as she pulled her bonnet off and ran her fingers through the braids, separating them. "Come on."

"Can I use the restroom up here?"

"Yeah, of course."

She left the bedroom and I moved into the bathroom. It was layered in stylish décor and I took a second to scan the area.

Two toothbrushes occupied a little holder resting on the sink. I opened the cabinet and looked at the items inside. Several of the little bottles read *Jason Van Noy*. Alprazolam, Zoloft, Prozac. Most of the bottles were very full and I wondered if Jace had been taking anything he was supposed to be.

I closed the cabinet and went to the bathroom. While washing my hands I splashed water on my face, looking at my tired eyes in the mirror. Apparently, one good night's sleep wasn't enough to erase the weeks of restlessness.

I headed downstairs and sat at the table in the breakfast nook of their kitchen. Riley moved around, starting the coffeemaker and pulling out a carton of eggs.

"Are you doing eggs these days?"

"I'm good—I'll just do a piece of toast," I said, pointing to the toaster on the counter.

She set a mug of coffee in front of me and turned back to the toaster. "There's creamer and everything in the fridge."

"Have you thought about going to a doctor or something? For the sleep, I mean?"

"Not really. I was thinking about going to this group thing, though. Like AA?"

"You have a drinking problem?"

She swiveled around to glare at me. "Johnny, I'm serious. It's for grief. A friend of mine told me about it. She went when she lost her sister and I thought maybe it would help? Would you want to go?"

Clearly whatever I had been doing so far wasn't working, as I was still seeing Dick everywhere I went. What would be the harm in trying this too?

"Yeah," I said, taking a sip of coffee. "I'd try it."

"Okay, great. I was planning on going to the meeting tomorrow. I'll text you the address."

"Great," I said, putting the cup back on the table.

"Have you been going to work?" she asked.

"Yeah."

"Is it weird?"

"A little."

"I'm there to keep you company," Dick said, resting his head against a wing at the table next to me.

"It does seem kind of stupid now, being there by myself. Going through all the motions like it's the same when we all know it's not. But at the same time, I'm also kind of tired of talking about it. You know?"

She laughed. "I do know. If one more person asks me if I'm okay, I'm going to lose my shit."

"Yeah, especially because you were never truly okay to begin with."

Turning, she smirked at me as the toaster finished its job.

"Alright, get your toast and get out."

I smiled as I stood to get my food. "What do you think Toni and Mark talk about when they're alone?"

"Do they even talk? I would guess they literally do anything they can to avoid being in the same space—that's why their house is so big?"

I laughed as I took a bite. "For sure. What is Barbara's boyfriend's name? I couldn't for the life of me remember it."

"I honestly don't remember. Are we sure he had a name?"

Slowly, I headed back to the empty table, listening to Riley hum as she cracked the egg on the side of the pan. We had never spent that much time together on our own without Jace involved. There was really no reason for us to. But it was nice, being with someone who understood.

5

SEASON 1 - EPISODE 5
The Side Quest

Mark stopped suddenly in the hallway, turning to me directly. "Are you sure you want to do this?"

"Yeah," I said with as much confidence as I could. The truth was I wasn't sure if I was mentally prepared for it or not, but it was happening regardless.

He started in on the process and what metrics were used and how they came to this conclusion and I only half listened, frankly uninterested on what words they put into a Word document that built the program to replace Jace.

"What's his name again?" I asked.

"David. David Owen."

I nodded. David Owen.

He was already in the booth when we entered the room.

Violet started messing with the controls and turned at the noise of the door.

"Guys, I told you—" she stopped when she saw me. "Oh my god, Johnny."

I moved forward to give her a hug.

"You okay?"

"Yeah," I said with the biggest smile I could muster. "I'm good. How are you?"

"We're trying. Take a seat."

I wanted to stand back in the corner, but both Violet and Mark motioned to the chair and I slid into it to watch David.

"Okay, David, we're going to run it again."

David nodded.

The light above him turned on and he leaned into the microphone. "It's not every day you get to see something so fucking stupid."

A chill ran through me as I turned to Violet. Her lips were drawn in a tight smile but her eyes betrayed her. It was weird.

"What the fuck," Dick said, standing on a chair next to me, straining to see the face of the man who sounded like a carbon copy of himself.

"How?" I asked.

"Crazy, isn't it?" Mark said, folding his hands across his chest.

"Why don't you call Eddie? Why don't you call Eddie? I already asked him twice; you're the one who doesn't want to admit it," David cried from the booth, altering his inflections as he repeated the phrases.

And then David laughed.

I stood up, sending the chair rolling behind me.

"I don't like this," Dick said, his little wings reaching up to grab his throat. "I'm not replaceable, you pieces of shit. You can't just hire someone else to say what I say. I'm one of a kind. I'm a product of my own creation. I'm not going to sit here and be artificially mimicked by this cheap little douchebag."

"I don't like this."

"Need a minute?" Mark asked, stepping toward me.

I suddenly didn't know why I had even agreed to join him. It was stupid to think this wasn't going to punch me in both my brain and stomach. I looked around for a trash can in case I threw up.

When I looked around, I didn't see any receptacle. All I saw were memories of sitting in the booth, listening to Jace put on a one-man show, loving every second of it.

"Go on," Violet said, raising the headphones back to her ears.

"I've done it six times now," Jace yelled from the other side.

"Do it right and then you won't have to do it another six."

"Yes, dear," he complied, reaching over to take a drink.

I shifted side-to-side in the chair, allowing my attention to be split between Jace in the booth and the call sheet on the laptop in front of me. Jace generally begged me to go with him to record and I always assumed it was so he could have an audience for how much he was fucking off rather than for any work related purpose.

He ran the lines two more times before Violet was satisfied.

"Okay, I'm taking a break."

Jace slipped his headphones off and grabbed his glass before heading into the control room.

"Are you drinking liquor at work?" I asked when I saw the amber liquid in the glass.

Jace shrugged and held it out in my direction. I grabbed it and smelled the overpowering smell of bourbon before I took a drink.

His eyes widened in delight. "I can't believe you did that."

"I'm full of surprises today," I said, turning back to my emails.

There was a knock at the door and all of us turned to see Evan waiting by the doorframe.

"What's up?" I asked, turning the chair to look at him directly.

He started in at a million miles a minute.

"Hold on," I stopped him. "I already sent out the call sheets for next week. You were on the email. Those are the times we've already set."

Evan turned to Jace expectantly.

Jace emptied his glass and set it on the small table behind me. "What the fuck are you looking at me for? He told you he already set the calls. If he said it, you do it. That's how this works."

"Okay, but—"

"I think you're still confused," Jace interrupted. "You're still talking to me about it. Am I in charge of calls?"

Evan turned to me and explained the scenario again. I could see him trying to weasel his way out of having to be ready to go at eight the morning he was needed. I wondered if Jace wasn't present if I would have caved. I went to college to write television and never imagined it would involve managing a team of writers like I knew what I was doing. Violet got up and headed out the door, understandably hoping to abandon what-ever was about to go down.

"Evan. Jesus. He's told you what's happening. He's your fucking boss. He sends out the call sheets and you show up to do your job. If that's a problem, you don't have to show up to anything ever again. Does that make sense?"

"Got it," he said abruptly before turning around and walking away.

"Can you seriously fire him, please?" Jace asked, leaning

forward to grab the glass and the bottle from the floor. I hadn't even noticed it before.

"Why do they listen to you?"

"Because I'm an asshole?" he said, taking a sip before inching the glass across the table in my direction. "You can't be an asshole though. They need someone to be nice to them. It only works with us both."

I took a drink and leaned back. "I didn't think this part of it through. The management part."

"Me either," he quipped, but I guessed that was probably a lie.

Jace was a natural born leader. He was better at directing things than knowing what actually needed to be done to achieve the goal. And though he would never admit it, I knew he loved it.

"Are you done for the day?" I asked as I eyed the glass.

He laughed and took one more sip before handing it over. "Don't be a party pooper."

"I'll report you to HR."

"I *am* HR," he challenged.

"Then I'd like to report a violation to you about you." I turned back to my computer to work on my actual work.

He laughed loudly again and stood up, reaching over to mess with my hair in the process. The touch of his hand on my scalp made my heart skip a beat. "Where did Violet go?"

Violet appeared next to me, looking concerned. "Are you alright?"

I looked back up and Jace was gone. Only David remained.

"Yeah. I'm fine."

Only I didn't think I was. I didn't think I was at all.

———

I looked around the faces sitting in a circle in the empty gymnasium. Most of the overhead lights were off and it was oddly comforting.

A few of them were speaking to one another—clearly well acquainted.

None of the faces belonged to Riley Van Noy. I pulled out my phone and was about to text her when a message came through. *I'm sorry, I can't make it tonight.*

I debated on cracking a joke, asking if she was okay or getting upset and ignoring it.

Everything okay? I responded.

I can't do it yet. I'm so sorry.

Totally understand. Let me know if you need anything?

The little bubble appeared before disappearing and no response came. I glanced around the group again. A few of them had begun looking in our—or my—direction.

"Tough crowd," Dick said next to me, pulling at his neck like a comedian.

Ignoring him, I took one of the empty chairs next to a woman who wasn't speaking to anyone. She was staring straight ahead as though in a trance. I continued to glance around the people. There was no rhyme or reason to them—all simply connected by loss. The only thing we all had in common was the absence in our lives.

"Hey." The woman started out of nowhere, drawing my attention to her.

"Hi," I said politely.

"I know you."

"Yeah?" I asked, unsure of where this was going.

"You wrote *Midnight Dolly*, didn't you?"

I nodded.

"I was on wardrobe. Your script was great. You're a wonderful writer."

"Thank you. What are you working on now?"

"*Pericles.*"

"Nice," I said, without any idea what that was.

There was a beat of silence before she offered a quiet, "I'm sorry about Jace."

"Yeah," I agreed. "Me too."

The woman sitting at what looked to be the head of the circle brought the group to order and began with a speech I imagined she gave at the top of every meeting. It was nice, comforting things about the room being safe to share the things that were holding us back, hurting us or simply impacting our day-to-day life.

She opened the floor for others to speak.

A man a few seats over began speaking about losing his father. He could barely get the words out through his tears. It made me angry to think that we lived our lives and connected so deeply to those around us, only to be separated so cruelly forever. I didn't believe in god and never had, but if I did, it would be one who relished the idea that we wanted to be together instead of punishing us and separating us forever with fire and brimstone.

Why would god create us with such a capacity to feel and then use that against us? It was too cruel to imagine. The reality was likely that we were all alone in the universe—incredible coincidences that emerged from mistakes and chance. And after every step worked piece-by-piece to create our world, we had to go and ruin it by inventing these systems of pain and punishment. It was actually insane.

Guilt...

Shame...

Pain...

What the fuck were we doing?

"I know I'll see him again," the man finished. "We'll be reunited in heaven."

Heaven...

If there was a heaven, Jace wasn't there.

And hell felt like where I was right now.

Was there somewhere in between perhaps? Somewhere we could exist on our own?

Everyone clapped and I joined in, looking at the faces around me—all as lost as me.

"We have some new faces here tonight. Would any of you like to speak?"

Everyone looked to me and one other person who must have also been new. The other person shook their head nervously.

"Would you like to speak?" the woman asked me.

"Sure," I said, surprising myself. "My name is Jonathan. Goodwin. I lost my best friend, Jason, or Jace. He went by Jace. We were... coworkers. But we were best friends before we were coworkers. I don't really know why I'm here. I feel... stuck... I guess. And thought maybe this would help. I can't move past him being gone, I guess."

"That goes away eventually," someone else offered. "It does take time."

I nodded.

"He, uh, he killed himself. Am I allowed to say that?"

The head lady nodded, her face lined with genuine sadness.

"Sorry, I don't mean to get weird about it, but you know, part of me feels like that's why I'm hung up maybe? Like it was so sudden and then he was just... gone. And it makes me so sad to think about him being in that kind of space mentally, you know?"

The group nodded and it was nice to think that we were all experiencing that kind of sadness together.

"I don't know. I'm sorry."

"You're not responsible," one of the men said from across the circle. "I know it may feel like that now, but you're not responsible."

"Sure," I offered.

I didn't think I was consciously thinking it as much now, but it was still there, in the back of my mind sometimes.

"I'm glad I showed up. I think this is great that you all help each other."

There were awkward smiles all around.

"Yuto?" the leader started. "Would you like to speak tonight?"

"My name is Yuto Tanaka."

"Hi Yuto," the group said together.

"Six years ago, I lost my wife, Eva. It was illness and probably the hardest thing I've ever been through in my life. The weeks without sleep, the guilt of being happy again, the balance of embracing her absence while creating a new future..."

Those around the circle were nodding with Yuto's story, seeing their own loss in his words.

"I feel like I'm in a good place these days, but I still like coming to this group. Mainly because of first timers, like Jonathan here, who have no one else to turn to. It really does make a difference to have someone on your side who knows what it's like. Your friends and family get it, but maybe not quite in the same way you do. But here we can be honest and make jokes and all of that is okay."

I smiled at his inclusion of *make jokes*. It was something Jace would have said.

I only half-listened to the rest of the group. The weight of what they were saying was starting to creep into my brain and while I had originally felt lighter after sharing, hearing their own grief felt like it was seeping into my own mind.

When the meeting was over, I had the urge to flee as fast as I could. Everyone began taking their chairs back to the rack against the wall. I joined in and when I turned around, Yuto was standing there, smiling.

"I'm glad you made it today. The first one is always the hardest," he said.

"Thanks. I'm sorry about your wife."

"Thank you. I'm sorry about Jace."

"Yeah, me too."

We stood there in silence, though it wasn't uncomfortable. The silence made me realize a certain little fowl was conspicuously absent. I looked around as subtly as I could, trying to see if Dick was lingering nearby.

"Are you looking for someone?" Yuto asked, matching my gaze around the room.

I shook my head. "No. Not at all."

He looked at me with a funny look on his face but said nothing, as though maybe he didn't believe me but wasn't going to make it an issue.

"I hope to see you at the next meeting. There's some statistic out there about the return rate of first time visitors."

"Really?"

"I'm sure there is somewhere." The edge of his mouth slid up slightly.

I laughed and it felt weird. Weird because it hadn't happened in a while, but also weird because I felt like I broke a rule or something. Yuto noticed and stepped forward a little bit.

"It's okay to laugh," he said. "I know sometimes you might feel like you need permission or something. But it's okay."

"Yeah?" I said, shifting uncomfortably. "You're right. Why is that?"

"The same reason you're holding your chest. It's pain."

I raised an eyebrow as I looked down at my hand, holding my body in comfort. I hadn't even realized I was. "Thanks."

"Of course. It is easier if you have someone who understands. Here," he said, pulling out his phone, "put your number in. I'll text you. That way if you need someone to talk to, you always have an option."

I followed his instructions before gently handing his phone back. My fingers brushed his as I did and I was surprised at how quickly my heart raced at the touch.

"It was nice to meet you, Jonathan."

"Johnny, actually. Everyone calls me Johnny."

"Got it. Nice to meet you, Johnny."

I smiled. "Nice to meet you too. Thank you."

I watched him leave and decided to not think through what it meant when I felt the little electric jolt inside when our fingers touched. Not that he wasn't an attractive man—he was —but it wasn't appropriate to think those kinds of things about random strangers you meet at grief clubs when they are there to grieve their wife.

I didn't feel like going home. But I didn't feel like going out either. I didn't feel like anything. Slowly, I walked toward my car trying to figure out where to go and what to do. With no Jace, no Blake and no direction of any kind, it was a concerning feeling to think about wandering from place to place, wasting time alone until I was needed somewhere else. There was no one to answer to and no one to make plans with. It had been a really long time since I felt so alone.

I pulled my car into the parking lot of Target and decided to wander around. The store was relatively empty inside and I aimlessly moved from aisle to aisle, looking at piles of late-stage capitalism and listening to the back and forth of those around me. It occurred to me that I was somehow trying to use the connection of strangers to feel something in my soul and it wasn't working. I still felt nothing.

"That's why I'm trying to hurry," a guy to my left said. "If we hurry here, I can make it work."

I listened to the sound of my shoes scraping the tile as I looked down the row of brightly colored candles.

"Stop!" a girl screeched as she pushed against the teenage boy teasing her.

All of them had lives, purpose, each other. And here I was, drifting through their reality, barely a part of the living, feeling nothing inside of me. I didn't even know where I was going or what I was looking for. I think I thought if I was around people I'd feel better, but honestly I felt so much worse.

My phone began buzzing in my pocket. I looked at the name: *Mom*.

"Hey," I answered, slowing my already slow pace to look at an end cap of candy.

"How are you? What are you doing?"

"I'm at Target," I said, hoping it sounded happier than I felt. "Just doing some shopping."

"That's good. I wanted to check in, see how you were doing."

"How are you?" I asked, resuming my shuffle toward the next aisle.

"I'm good. We went to the fish shack today. It's been raining all week."

"That's too bad. About the rain, I mean."

"Yeah, but we need it."

The corner of my mouth turned up. Every time she called it was either raining cats and dogs or dry as a desert and killing everything. I wondered if she had thought up things to say about the weather before calling so we'd have something to talk about.

"How is the weather there?" she asked.

"Dry. Warm."

"That's nice."

"Mmhmm," I said, turning down an aisle of doormats. I had a doormat, but couldn't remember ever buying one. Maybe I needed a new one.

After a beat of silence she started in again. "When are you going to be able to come visit us? It would be nice to see you, see how you are."

I could hear the concern in her voice. "Yeah, it would be good to see you. I probably can. Soon, I'm sure."

"Are you sleeping?"

"Yeah," I lied.

"And eating?"

I looked down at the bottle of wine in my basket. "Yes."

"More than chips?"

"Yes."

She sighed. "I'm so worried about you. Being alone."

"I'm fine, Mom."

"You should bring Riley. You and Riley should come visit."

"She'd like that. I'll ask her."

"Promise?"

"Yeah, I promise."

There was another beat of silence as I stared at a doormat with the words *so happy you're here* printed on it. I reached out to touch it and felt the scratchy threads on my fingertips. I knew Mom only liked Riley because it was always proof to her that Jace and I weren't dating. Surprisingly never for homophobic reasons, but because my mother had absolutely never trusted Jace and often told me he was, in her words, "bad news."

"How is she handling things?"

"About as well as she can, I guess. We had dinner the other night and she's okay."

I left out the part that she couldn't sleep because when she closed her eyes all she saw was the face of her dead husband staring back at her.

"And how are you handling things?"

"You know. Some days are better than others."

More silence.

"I, uh, actually went to a grief meeting tonight. I think that will help."

"Oh," she said as though she was surprised.

She didn't believe in things like therapy, or counseling. Like all emotions, grief was bottled away, dealt with at a different time. When her mother died, she seemed to just carry on, like nothing happened.

"It will get better, with time," she offered.

"Yeah, thanks."

"I watched that movie you told me about with that one boy —the gay one."

"The gay one?" I laughed lightly. "Did you like it?"

"It was alright. Kind of sad."

I didn't even know which movie she was talking about. All movies were sad to her, especially the gay ones.

"Oh, honey, I've got to go. Scamp is scratching at the door."

"Alright Mom. I love you."

"I love you too. Call me soon?"

"I will."

The hum of the line stopped as we were cut off from each other. I slipped my phone in my pocket and looked back to the doormat.

"Do you think she's sad that you're gay?" Dick asked at my feet.

"I don't know."

"You know she is."

"Then why did you ask?"

"To see if you'd admit it."

"Admitting things to myself has never been my strong suit," I mumbled as I reached out and pulled the mat from the shelf. If nothing else, I knew I could at least get small hit of dopamine from buying it.

That's I all I was chasing now anyways—small little micro transactions in my brain that reminded me once and for all that I was alive, just like everyone else.

"I'm so happy *you're* here," Dick said as I tucked the mat under my arm.

"Come on," I said reluctantly. "Let's go home."

I headed to the front of the store, listening to the little webbed feet pitter-patter on the glossy tile behind me.

6

SEASON 1 - EPISODE 6
Jumping the Shark

I woke up and checked my phone, only realizing after the fact that I had slept the entire night without waking up once.

One of the text notifications caught my eye. It was Yuto.

I'm an idiot, it started, causing me to smile. *You're the creator of the tv show* Dick? *You didn't say anything about any of that!*

It made me feel warm and fuzzy inside at the realization that the only way he would have found out if he didn't know before was that he was looking for me online. I reminded myself that he had a dead *wife* and pushed away any butterflies. For a brief moment, I began to worry he was going to be weird about the Hollywood aspect of it all. On more than a few occasions I had met strangers who acted like they had no idea who I was until they were suddenly submitting audition tapes and headshots.

I debated my response for a moment.

That's just my day job.

He laughed at that.

What do you do for work? I asked.

He replied quickly: *I'm retired. I created a company out of college and sold it to ensure I would never have to work again unless I wanted to.*

Impressive! I replied, hoping it didn't sound too flirty. I never knew how to actually flirt with men. And not that I was trying, but maybe in some ways I really was.

Not quite as impressive as being nominated for an Emmy.

Which is also not as impressive as "winning" an Emmy.

He sent a laughing emoji and I locked my phone before pulling myself out of bed. For the first time in a long time, I felt like I could potentially complete at least one, maybe even two of the tasks I had on my growing to-do list. It was dumb, but having little butterflies in my stomach felt nice and it had been ages since I had felt like that about anyone.

I showered quickly and started to get ready for a long day at the office. When I wiped the condensation from the mirror, Dick was there, waiting.

"Why are you whistling? What the fuck happened to you?"

"I'm in a good mood. Isn't that allowed?"

"Because of the guy from the meeting? He said he had a dead wife. What the fuck. You know how creepy that is? To hit on every straight guy you see just because you think they're cute?"

"I wasn't hitting on him."

"But you want to. You want to fuck Yuto, don't you?"

"God," I started, putting toothpaste on my toothbrush. "Can't you please shut up for a minute and let me have this?

You're so fucking loud sometimes. I'm allowed to think he's hot."

"He's probably straight and probably thinks that's gross."

"Now you're being dumb," I replied as I brushed my hair. "Not everyone is homophobic."

"Most people are, when it comes down to it. They might praise you to your face but they think you're a biological freak behind your back. You know there's no social reason for gays to exist? Like you, have you—"

I pulled out my phone and started my music, playing David Bowie as loud as I could and shutting Dick in the bathroom behind me as I went to get dressed.

At the office, I threw my bag down on the desk and listened as Annie shuffled over.

"How are you this morning?" she asked with a smile.

I smiled back and felt a little swell in my heart as I realized it was genuine and not forced.

"I'm actually good, I think. How are you?"

"I'm great. I have some good news for you."

"Oh?" I asked, arranging my laptop and mouse pad in neat little rows. Jace always mocked me to no end that everything on my desk had to be in the exact right place all the time. But on the flip side, he spent far too long looking for a single piece of paper because he had no clue where anything was—ever.

"Emmy noms are for sure hitting Thursday."

"Is that good news?"

She huffed and moved closer. "This is going to be it. I can feel it. My reading this weekend saw a golden statue."

I laughed and looked up at her very serious brown eyes watching me carefully. "Listen, if you believe in *Dick*, I believe in you."

She jumped back and practically bounced out of the room. "Let me know if you need anything."

"What was that about?" Jace asked, walking in and putting a pizza box and Styrofoam container on top of my desk.

"Really?" I asked, annoyed, moving it to readjust my computer and everything underneath it.

Jace paused to watch what I was doing before slumping into the seat across from me. "Seriously with your rearranging shit?"

"Just because you like chaos doesn't mean I have to," I mumbled.

"Fair enough." He leaned forward and pulled a piece of pizza out of the box. "Eat please. I got you that nasty salad you like. You're still vegetarian these days?"

"Yes. Thank you."

I took the takeout container and began picking at the lettuce, while Jace started in on some weird interaction he had while buying the pizza that was sure to become a bit in the next season of the show. He talked with his mouth full, like a child.

Barbara appeared in the doorway of the office, looking down at Jace.

"Barbara," I said, surprised. "What are you doing here?"

"I've been trying to get ahold of this asshole all day," she said, pointing to Jace. "Why won't you answer my calls? Did you say Keanu Reeves was a piece of shit on Instagram?"

"Does that really sound like something I would say?" Jace asked, taking another bite of pizza.

"Yes," Barbara and I answered in unison.

"Come on," he started, leaning back and raising his hand. "You know it's true. Someone *should* say it. Someone who is definitely not me, but someone else with an Internet platform, should."

"Literally everyone else on the planet knows that's not true. You know I have other clients, right? I shouldn't need to spend all of my time chasing you down and apologizing for your dumb ass."

"Then don't," he said, shrugging. "Get the fuck out. I won't pay you anymore to apologize for me."

She stopped talking and looked at him in shock.

"Guys," I started, trying to keep the peace.

"No, Johnny, he's right. I've put up with this shit for long enough. I'm out. You can find someone else willing to take on your stupid risky ass."

"Bye, Barbara!" he cried, standing up. "I'm deleting your phone number, Barbara!"

He yelled this down the hall and I could see a few employees looking from the stomping Barbara to the screaming Jace and back and forth and back and forth.

"What are you doing?" I asked, rubbing my temple.

"What? Seriously? Like I should just take that?"

"You were antagonizing her."

"Me?" he scoffed, raising both hands to his chest.

"How many times did she call you today?"

"I don't know. I don't have my phone on me," he grumbled as he reached for another piece of pizza from the box.

"Just call her. Apologize. Please."

"Do I have to?" he whined like a toddler.

"Yes. Now, actually."

"Fine, *Mom*."

He dropped the pizza back on the top of the box and dragged his feet dramatically out of the office. I could hear him get his phone from his desk.

"No, I didn't delete your number," I heard him start. "I'm sorry, I'm being a dick today. Do you forgive me?"

He walked back in with the phone cradled to his ear and gave me a thumbs up.

"I said I'm sorry. Yes, Johnny made me call you, but I chose to actually do it. I love you. I'm sorry. I'm the worst."

He hung up and plopped back down in the chair before picking up his slice. "Happy?"

"Yes. Thank you."

I leaned back in my chair. "Did you really call Keanu Reeves a piece of shit on Instagram?"

He shook his head emphatically between bites. "Twitter."

I tried to keep a stern face, but couldn't help it. He knew it would get me and we both laughed so hard, mine turned into a silent wheeze.

"I don't even know why I try. He's actually the nicest person—you're going to hell for that one."

"Well, I'll see him there. Listen, I've got to go record at two and I want you to go with me," he said, looking at his phone and standing. "Will you please actually eat some food and be ready to go by then?"

"Sure, Dad."

He left the office and Annie was standing there when he walked out.

"What's up?"

"They're waiting for you in the conference room. Were you going to the writing meeting?"

I looked down at my desk and realized where I was in my life. Dick sat in the chair Jace had vacated, watching me carefully. There was no pizza box on top of my computer.

"Are you losing your mind?" Dick asked quietly.

"Yeah," I said, standing and grabbing my notebook. "I'm ready. Let's go."

I could see everyone sitting and waiting from the big glass wall that led into our main writer's room. I had the meeting written down for eleven; I didn't know how I lost track of time.

"Sorry I'm late," I said, pushing open the door. It fell shut too quickly for Dick to enter and he stood at the door, beating loudly on the glass.

"Alright, who wants to start?" I asked, trying desperately to ignore Dick's frantic banging.

"We're on episode seven today," Mason said at the head of the table.

Everyone began clicking on their laptops and opening their notebooks. Mason continued, in true Executive Producer form. I wasn't really needed for these kinds of meetings anymore, but I felt like lately that I was doing the bulk of the show-running on my own, it would help to hit every writing meeting I could.

My vision was interrupted by Dick smashing through the glass wall with a sledgehammer much too large for him to hold in his feathery hands. He glared at me as he marched in and plopped himself at the table across from me.

"Can we revisit the Clem conversation?" Trax asked.

"No," Dick said from across the room.

"No," I replied.

"Why not?"

I looked in Dick's direction, waiting for his answer and noticed that Trax slowly followed my gaze to the empty wall.

"Clem isn't enough of a foil. If we're going to bring in a secondary, it should be comic relief only."

"Clem isn't enough of a foil," I started. "If we're going to bring in a secondary, it should be funny."

"Comic relief!" Dick yelled. "There's a difference!"

"That's what I said."

Everyone turned to look at me as I realized I had answered Dick out loud.

"Last month, I mean, that's originally what I said."

Mason looked over with one raised eyebrow, but said nothing.

"Then what are we going to do for Act Three?"

"You're the fucking writers!" Dick yelled, climbing up on top of the table. "All you can come up with is fucking Clem?"

"How about death?" I asked, looking Dick right in the eyes. "What if we killed him? Or better yet, what if Dick killed himself?"

The room fell silent as I realized the weight of what I had said.

"Fuck," Dick offered, disgusted at us. "Read the room, brother."

"Hey, Johnny, can I speak to you? Outside?" Mason asked.

"Sure," I said, standing, knowing what was coming.

The room was deathly quiet and even Dick shut his fucking beak as he watched us leave with eyes wider than he had ever been drawn.

"What was that?" Mason asked in the hallway as soon as the door had closed.

"What was what?" I asked, stupidly.

"John, come on."

"I didn't mean it. It was..." I looked back in the room, knowing I couldn't explain how I wanted Dick to die, not my creation and not the memory of Jace or whatever manifestation the show had now taken.

Dick was marching up and down the table, kicking little animated papers as he did, yelling and pointing like a televangelist. There was no telling what he was saying. His brow was drawn in a straight line to emphasize his fury of impending fire and brimstone. Hell hath no fury like a duck ignored.

"Johnny," Mason said louder, drawing my attention back. "Maybe it's too soon to be here. Why don't you take the day off?"

I shook my head. "No, I'm good. I'm sorry. I won't make any references to death or suicide."

Glancing back into the room, Dick had moved to the head

of the table and was wrapping a noose around his neck. "Okay." I threw up my hands in defeat.

"What?" Mason asked, looking back into the room and back to me. "What is going on, man? Are you okay?"

"Yeah, actually, I think you're right. I need some fresh air."

"Okay. Do you want someone to go with you?"

"No," I shook my head. "I'm good. Just need a minute."

Mason patted my shoulder awkwardly as we turned to go back into the room. When he opened the glass door, I was glad to hear the low murmurs of actual conversation though there was a pause as we returned. There was no sign of Dick and I relaxed a bit as I moved toward my seat to gather my things. When I turned around the corner of the table, I saw him sprawled comically on the floor, his eyes now large X's across his face and the sight made me laugh out loud. It was funny, really—death in general, but also the idea of Dick killing himself after Jace had. It would have been funny in the show too. Like I kind of thought maybe audiences would appreciate that we killed Dick when Jace killed himself. Like maybe they would get it, that Dick couldn't survive outside of Jace's voice and mind and Dick had to kill himself to let Jace go once and for all. They would have gotten it. I got it.

"Dude," Kenny said. "Are you alright?"

"Yeah, sorry," I attempted to recover, knowing that walking into a room and laughing after they were already all concerned about my mental health wasn't really a good look.

But it *is* a good joke, I thought. And I saw Dick smile from the floor.

SEASON 1 - EPISODE 7
Cousin Oliver

When Barbara called, she seemed annoyed, and while it wasn't unusual for her to be annoyed, it was unusual for her to summon me to the board-walk of Santa Monica Boulevard like we were going on a picnic date without any explanation of why.

I tried to think of why we were meeting clandestinely in the park like two spies in a cheap network thriller, but couldn't reason it away. Despite trying to arrive a little late, knowing she would be at least fifteen minutes later than that, I got there early and decided to pace up and down the street until she arrived.

"Are you trying to kill me?" Dick cried as he struggled to keep up with my long stride.

"I would if I could," I said with indignation. "Is this annoying? You having to walk so much behind me?"

"I'm not real, I don't get tired," he barked.

"Could I kill you?" I asked, turning once more. "I hadn't really thought about it, but surely there's a way to kill you."

I checked the time again as Dick continued on, mumbling about creative license and artistic integrity—whatever that meant. Barbara's car pulled up in the lot across the crossway from the beach.

I watched her as she carefully got out of her car and adjusted her sunglasses before reaching down to grab two cups of coffee. She scanned the walkway and I raised my hand so she could see me. Bobbing in acknowledgment, she headed our way.

Barbara handed over one of the cups of coffee as she approached. I noticed the name *Barbara* written on it.

"Your parents really looked at you in the hospital as a little baby and named you Barbara?"

Dick laughed next to me.

She scrunched her nose in annoyance before taking a drink. "Yeah? So?"

"It's such an old lady name," I teased.

Both her hands flew up and I marveled that her coffee didn't spill. It always annoyed me in TV shows when actors tossed around coffee cups that were clearly never filled with liquid. No one did that in real life. "What do you want me to do? Change my name so I don't sound like a grandma to you? It was my Bubbe's name so what can I do about that?"

I smiled as we resumed walking down the sidewalk. Irritating Barbara was one of my favorite pastimes.

"You're one to talk, Jonathan Goodwin. Your name sounds like a freaking sports player from the thirties."

"What?" Dick quacked. "That doesn't even make sense."

I agreed with Dick, but Barbara was an agent and not a writer, so I kept my mouth shut.

"So, why are we out here on Santa Monica Boulevard like you're about to tell me my sweet little puppy went to live on my Uncle Milo's farm?"

"Listen, there's no easy way to say this so I'll lay it out. They are bringing in a show runner, Christian Wiley, for *Dick*. They thought it would be easier coming from me."

"What?" I stopped in my tracks. "Why?"

"You really don't know why?" Dick asked. "You're fucking it all up. You're ruining our show. That's why."

It was Jace's voice that yelled at my feet.

"It's been a lot for you to handle on your own. It could be a good thing. This could be good. You get some space and time away from the show. And you can pursue other things in the meantime. I get calls every day for people who want your material. Maybe it's time you broke up with Dick a little bit. I know it was your and Jace's baby, but now it's just not going to be the same for you."

I made a noise that was supposed to be a laugh, but came out more like a cough.

She sighed heavily and shielded her eyes, despite wearing sunglasses. "Johnny, I'm really sorry. I didn't know how you'd take it."

"I don't have a choice, I guess. Send me something else. If you're really getting calls about my work, let's set up a few meetings. I can't not work right now."

She nodded. "Lee Young has called me ten times now trying to get you in a room. Want it?"

"Sure. I like Lee. Why didn't she call me herself? We know each other."

Barbara shrugged. "I don't know how this business really works when it comes down to it."

"You can say that again," Dick jeered.

"Do I get to meet with him?" I asked.

"Who?"

"Wiley. I want to meet with him. He's not even a writer. How is he going to know anything?"

"He's got the bible and access to everything in the production team."

"Not my brain. My brain is the show."

"Literally," Dick quacked.

I glared down at him before I could stop myself.

Barbara followed my glance before turning her face back to me. "I'll see what I can do."

I laughed out loud this time, knowing the anger was bubbling up and I couldn't stop it.

"You'll see what you can do? I'm having my work stripped from me and you'll *see what you can do?*"

"Come on. Don't make it like this."

Biting my tongue, I held my hand up more to calm myself than anything else. "Please. Get me a meeting with Wiley about Dick and Lee about new work. I appreciate it. And you."

She awkwardly reached out to touch my arm. "I'm sorry."

"It's not your fault. Sorry I got angry."

"It's alright. I'll call you when I know something."

She started to walk away before I stopped her. "Hey, remember that time Jace tried to fire you? I was thinking about that the other day."

Her eyebrows drew together and she raised her hand to her sunglasses. "What? When?"

"I think it was last year some time. You guys got in this big fight."

It looked like she was really trying to remember, but couldn't. "Yeah, I guess. I don't remember that. You'd think that would be something I'd remember. I'll call you soon, Johnny."

I hadn't imagined that, had I?

She trudged away and I stood there, stupidly, with Dick at my feet. My brain returned to my problem at hand. I hadn't considered the idea that I wouldn't be able to manage the show on my own. And if I was being honest, as the shock wore off, I thought I felt a modicum of relief. My eyes fell on a bench nearby and I took off for it. By the time I reached it, I looked around and realized I was alone.

I scanned the area for signs of my little duck shadow, but all I could see were happy beach goers, going about their day without a care in the world. Where had he gone?

As I sat, I pulled out my phone and Googled Christian Wiley. He looked like he was about twenty and his credits were short. What qualified him to take over our show?

"Nothing," Dick answered, suddenly next to me on the bench. "They are Cousin Olivering Jace."

My eyes snapped from the phone to the duck who had suddenly reappeared.

"Stop." I turned my attention back to the phone and scrolled over the pictures of the little kid. He was so young.

"In case you don't know, when a show is dying, they bring a young replacement for the lead to pull in a new generation like Chachi on Happy Days. Did it start with Chachi or...?"

"Brady Bunch," I corrected myself. "You know that. It's called Cousin Oliver, not Cousin Chachi. Why am I arguing with you? And why are you explaining it to me? We know this."

"I'm explaining to the audience," Dick said angrily. "Not everybody knows TV tropes like you."

"What audience?" I looked up at the cartoon duck and around us on the empty beach.

Dick crossed his wings and stared straight into the camera. *Sheesh.*

"Okay, stop, Jesus." I stood. "Come on. We need food and probably alcohol."

"Yes!" Dick cried, jumping up and down as he waddled behind. "We love alcohol."

"Yeah," I resigned. "Yeah, we do."

I walked into one of the trendy bars on the pier and nearly laughed at the idea. A sad gay writer day-drinking to mourn the loss of their television show seemed more cliché than I could possibly imagine and I angrily decided if god was a writer, they were a pretty shitty one.

I ordered a beer and watched Dick struggle to climb up onto the stool using nothing but wings and little webbed feet. He tried a few times to pull up his oddly shaped body using his feathers but kept sliding down. Then he tried running and jumping, flapping madly to try and gain enough height to get into the stool.

"Will you help me?!" he screamed.

"I can't help you. You aren't real. I can't pick you up."

The bartender wasn't near enough to hear, but did look over at the noise, which surprised me that he could hear anything over Joe Cocker crooning overhead. I took another long drink of my beer and kept watching Dick struggle with the stool. It was oddly therapeutic.

"What are you chasing away today?" the bartender asked, as he swept the rag across the bar top near me.

"Oh, well, you know, my best friend killed himself a few weeks ago and I lost my job today. I was replaced, which oddly feels worse than straight up being fired. My boyfriend left me a few weeks ago. Right after my friend died, actually, which was really pretty shitty?"

"Oh," was all they said in response.

"Too much?" I asked, before finishing the beer.

"Here," he said, pushing another one forward. "This one's on me."

Dick had made it to the top of the stool and laughed maniacally before throwing back a shot of what looked to be tequila. "Oh my god, you have touristy bartenders feeling so sorry for you they are offering free beer. How does that not just crush any hope you had left for being a normal fucking person?"

I pulled out my phone, trying desperately to figure out a plan. Dick was right—*of course I'm right*—I was verging on a crash. So far I had been doing a good job of pushing and pushing everything out of my brain when it felt like it was getting too crowded, but there was a limit to what I could push and it was about to crack my mind for good.

Hey, I texted Yuto. *I know it's last minute, but I got some bad news at work today and could use someone to talk to. Are you busy?*

Not at all. Want to meet somewhere?

I looked down at the full glass of beer in front of me and decided against alcohol.

Coffee?

Absolutely.

Dialog Café?

His response buzzed in my fingers as I second-guessed even asking him in the first place. I looked at the text, examining each letter like it would reveal something new.

That sounds fun. I'll see you soon.

Fun? F u n ? FUN.

f

u

n?

Was I dumb?

"You're really questioning whether or not you're dumb?

You just asked a straight man on a date. A straight man who lost his wife to cancer."

"It wasn't cancer," I muttered, pulling out some cash and putting it on the bar. It was more than enough to pay for both beers.

"Thank you!" I called to the bartender who had moved to the other side of the bar to the only other person present.

It took me thirty minutes to get to the coffee shop and I waited in my car for the remaining twenty until I saw Yuto walking across the street. I got out and headed toward him with a smile.

"Thanks for meeting me."

"Of course," he offered, reaching out for a hug. "I've never tried this place before. I'm excited to try it."

It felt weird to hug him and I was aware I was being overly self-conscious about it.

We continued the idle chit-chat as we made our way inside and I marveled at how easy it was to talk to him. I had only known him for a few weeks but it felt like we had been friends for years. It was difficult, making friends as an adult, and things were so easy with Yuto.

"What is your go-to?" he asked as he looked at the menu.

"I'm a firm flat white drinker."

He nodded while still looking at the menu. "Noted."

I smiled as I stepped forward to order before waving him forward.

"No, that's okay."

"Come on, I invited you, let me get your coffee."

He obliged and ordered before moving to get us a table outside on the patio.

"So, what's the bad news? Are we here to talk about Jace or you or none of the above?"

"Well, work, but that involves Jace and me, honestly."

Yuto smiled in return and when he did, I noticed that one side of his mouth rose higher than the other. It was incredibly charming.

"Hit me."

"They hired a show runner to take over *Dick*."

"Do we hate them?" he asked.

I laughed as a waiter brought out our drinks and set them down. Once they were gone, I began to explain. "I don't hate him. I think it'd be easier if I could honestly. He seems nice. Eager. It's just so weird to think of someone else taking over what we spent so much time and effort on. Like, he wasn't there when we hit all of our milestones and wrote our first episode and watched it air on national television. He's going to make it his thing now. It won't even involve us."

"Do you think it would mean the same to you without Jace involved?"

"Probably not, realistically."

"I don't really know anything about TV, so sorry if this is a stupid question, but will you still be involved at all?"

"On a large scale. Like for promotion and stuff like that. The network knows if both Jace and I are gone from it, we lose viewers. I'm still a writer, I think? They haven't told me I'm not. But, I don't know, it feels like it's getting further and further away from me."

He nodded. "It's not the same, but after Eva died, our mutual hobbies seemed to lose all interest to me. Like doing that thing without her seemed kind of empty."

"Exactly."

"I don't know how that would feel though for you and the show. I don't know."

I took a drink before getting the courage to ask. "Have you seen it?"

Yuto's face flushed as he grinned like he'd been caught in

the middle of something. "I hadn't... but once I found out who you were, I started watching it. And then watched, like, all of it. It's really good."

I laughed out loud. "Well, thanks."

"It must be weird, putting something so personal out there for the world to enjoy."

"Yeah, a little."

A lot, actually, but I didn't want to admit that. Especially when people hated it and told me they hated it online.

"I guess I thought with your history and your company you might have some insight or something into what it feels like to watch someone slowly take over the thing you spent so much time creating."

He nodded and took a sip. "For sure. I mean, I definitely struggled at first. Both from the lack of having something to do, and also from telling myself that I didn't need to be involved or make decisions anymore. It's really hard. But honestly, I had to trust that if I felt I made the decision that it was the right one."

"That's the thing, I didn't make this decision. It's being taken from me."

"It still might be the right one. Maybe it wouldn't be a bad thing to give yourself some space to breathe from Jace and all of those memories?"

"Sure." I looked at my leg bobbing up and down. "I think maybe there is a part of me that resents the show, and maybe even Jace."

"That's normal."

"Like he up and left me with this shit show and now I can't even handle it."

"I think you're being pretty hard on yourself."

I laughed.

"One thing someone told me when I was debating on selling or not was that, regardless, I should be proud that I

"Sure." Books were safe. Books would give us something to do and prevent me from being as awkward as possible.

He slipped his arm through the crook of mine as we crossed the street and I did everything I could to stop the smile from sticking on my face.

———

When I closed my front door, my eyes fell on Dick, sitting in the chair in the front room, wings crossed, glaring angrily. I dropped my newly acquired stack of books on the entryway table and pulled my shoes off.

"Where do you think you've been, young man?"

"What?" I asked, confused.

"I've been waiting here for hours."

"No you haven't."

I headed into the kitchen and opened the fridge, scanning the empty shelves for anything edible. Settling for a can of Diet Coke, I closed the fridge and Dick was standing on the other side, still glaring.

"What the hell?" I asked, staring down at him.

"I've been worried sick about you."

"No. You haven't."

I pushed past him and headed for the stairs. I was actually tired, both mentally and physically and for once, ready for bed. Dick was yammering behind me but I barely heard him as I changed clothes and brushed my teeth. I plopped into bed and pulled out my phone, scrolling through social media. Dick stopped talking and I lowered my phone down to make sure he was still there. He was staring at the wall like he was stuck in some kind of glitch.

"What the hell are you doing?"

He didn't respond and I scrunched my face in confusion. I

created something to sell. And you should be too. You should be proud of this insanely crazy thing you created."

I was positive my ears were burning; I knew my face was flushed, and I wanted to do anything possible to change the subject. The universe intervened as I looked behind Yuto to see Blake and another man walking up the street. The man looked shockingly like me. It had to be the new boyfriend. I rescinded my previous dig at god for their shitty writing abilities.

"Jesus," I exhaled, eyes fixed on them approaching.

"Who is it?" Yuto asked without looking, realizing that I was watching someone behind him.

"My ex-boyfriend, actually, and probably his current boyfriend?"

"Ah," he said, leaning forward to get his coffee. "How do you want to play it? Madly-in-love? First date?"

"What?" I asked with a laugh of concern and confusion. "What are you talking about?"

Before he could answer, Blake was close enough on the sidewalk to make eye contact and I couldn't help but look at him as he arrived. "Johnny?"

I raised a hand in a friendly wave.

"How's it going?" he asked as he approached.

"Hey there," I replied, standing. He moved forward and opened his arms as though expecting a hug.

Yuto stood before I could reciprocate, moving next to me and sticking out his hand. "I'm Yuto."

"Blake," he replied, looking Yuto up and down.

"Is that...?" I asked, looking toward the man following up behind him.

"Yeah," Blake replied, almost looking embarrassed. "That's Chandler."

I was shocked to see how much Chandler looked like me. I

never took Blake for having a type, but the resemblance seemed too odd to be coincidence.

"Blake is my ex-boyfriend," I said, turning to Yuto. "And Chandler is who he left me for."

"It wasn't like that," Blake said quickly.

"Well, I'm grateful," Yuto started. "If you hadn't, I would have never gotten my chance."

I turned slowly to look at Yuto, who grinned a wide grin, and I could practically see the little hearts in his eyes. I couldn't tell if I wanted to laugh or die of embarrassment right on the spot. Maybe both?

"Oh?"

"Oh yeah," Yuto said, slipping his arm through mine. "He's so great. I can't believe I lucked out with him."

"Yeah," Blake said, "he's definitely great."

Chandler had watched the whole exchange silently, but moved closer at Blake's compliment of me, sensing the need for him to assert his territory if needed.

"It was good to see you," I said, wanting the entire exchange to be over.

Blake raised his hand in farewell and continued on with Chandler. Yuto still had his arm wrapped through mine and I attempted to pull away, but he stuck to me.

"They might still be watching," Yuto said quietly as he laughed loudly at something I didn't say.

"What are you doing?" I asked, now laughing genuinely.

Yuto moved around the table to sit, pulling me down with him as he refused to let go of my arm.

"What was that?" I asked nervously, when he finally let go. He was sitting so close his knee was touching mine under the little bistro table.

"I've always wanted to do that," Yuto said, eyes glistening in excitement.

"Do what? Pretend to be gay?"

He laughed a high-pitched laugh and leaned forward. "No, silly, make someone jealous by pretending to be their partner. Fake dating."

"Yeah? That's very TV tropey of you."

Yuto nodded before taking a drink. "I know. It's hilarious."

"I don't know if we know each other well enough for me to say this, but for what it's worth you play a pretty good fake boyfriend."

"Thank you," he said, flattered. "I've been told I play pretty good real boyfriend too."

"Impressive. Do you currently have a real girlfriend?" asked offhandedly as I took a sip.

"No girlfriend or boyfriend at the moment."

"Oh," I said, surprised as my heart started to race in chest. I needed to stop drinking coffee in the after "Okay. So…"

"Yes," he drew out again. "I had a wife. And before had boyfriends. And girlfriends. Bisexuals do exist, Johnn

"No, I know, I didn't mean," I started and he bur laughter at my awkwardness.

"I know."

"Well, I don't currently have a boyfriend either, putting my cup down in front of me.

An awkward silence settled between us and I trie as I could to think of anything that didn't somehow so was trying to hit on him.

"Okay. I'm out of things to talk about apparently.

"We don't have to talk," he said. "Want to take a

"Yes, please," I said quickly.

He laughed and stood, waiting for me to step we took off in the opposite direction that Blake was

"Book Soup?" he asked, pointing.

followed his eye line to the box that had been resting on the floor since I put it there, weeks ago. Something in my brain remembered the odd legal envelope I had stuffed inside and my curiosity got the best of me.

Forgetting Dick for a moment, I pulled myself out of bed and moved over to the box, plopping onto the ground.

"What are you doing?" Dick asked, suddenly next to me, his wings cradling his head as he rested on his stomach as though nothing had happened.

"Going through some shit."

I opened the box and began pulling out pieces of Jace, tossing them on the floor next to me. Dick reached over and grabbed the little duck, staring into its eyes like he was having some kind of animated existential crisis.

After finding the envelope in question, I dragged it out and put it in my lap, debating for the first time if it was the right thing to do or not. Part of me guessed it wasn't, as Jace was dead and this was personal and if he had wanted me to see it, he would have shown me. But the other part of me realized that if there *was* something legally wrong with Jace, it would be good for me to know, since we were pretty legally bound together. And the final part of me had this deep feeling of dread, thinking that whatever the envelope held might have some kind of direct connection to the reason Jace was currently dead.

"Just open it," Dick said from the floor, more defeated than I had ever heard him.

I pulled at the top of the envelope and let the paper fall to my lap.

To Jason Van Noy, it started. My eyes began scanning the paper and at first when my eyes read *copyright infringement* I felt a bit of relief. We fought copyright infringement cases all day long when people put their own versions of Dick online or used clips in their videos without paying us a single dime. I didn't give a shit, but it was something the studio was pretty stuck on in general.

But then I kept reading and realized it wasn't for Dick, it was against Dick. Dick was the infringement.

"My client," it read, "has shared with me substantial evidence..."

Stolen, it claimed.

Dick was stolen property.

Damages.

Copyright infringement.

Stolen. Fraud. Fake.

"You stole him?" I managed to ask out loud.

Dick gasped in angst. "I knew you weren't my real fathers."

"God damn it, Jace. What the hell did you do?"

Without realizing it, I let myself fall backwards to the floor. Dick climbed up on my stomach and began slapping my face.

"Stay with me, Johnny. I'm right here, buddy. I'm right here."

I laughed, loudly, letting the sound become as maniacal as it possibly could as every piece of emotion I had bottled up for years came pushing through to the surface.

"But you're not!" I yelled. "You're actually not. I'm here. And I'm going to have to deal with this. And you're just fucking gone. You fucking bounced, you goddamn piece of shit."

Closing my eyes, I pushed my fingers into my eyes trying to organize my thoughts into what I would have to do. The first was Riley. The fact that the envelope was at the office made me guess there was no way Riley actually knew what it said. And I was going to have to be the one to tell her about it. And then Barbara. And our lawyer. And it was going to cost us so much fucking money. And we'd probably lose the show. This was going to kill *Dick*.

I opened my eyes and stared at the ceiling, thinking about

the first time I met Jace. I don't know why, but that first class we had together was stuck in my brain, replaying over and over as the fan spun around and around like time winding back and forth and back and forth. Like it was happening now like it happened then.

"Partners?" he had asked. The first words he ever spoke to me.

It was my first screenwriting class in college. The room was stuffy and filled with aspirational idiots, waiting to get through this part of things to get to the point where they got their big break. The professor, who had long given up on any hope of getting his own chance to put anything he wanted to out into the world, called for us to partner up and review each other's scripts.

Jace leaned over his desk in my direction, waiting for my answer.

"Sure," I replied, suddenly nervous at the idea of someone reading my writing.

I had done everything possible to avoid sharing my stuff. Slowly, I handed over my pages, feeling the sweat mounting on the back of my neck. If he hated it and laughed at me, I'd have to drop the class.

He pushed his papers across the desk and shuffled down in his seat as he read. I started in on his, but looked up when I heard him laugh. His blue eyes were trailing along the page, crinkling at the edges as he read. He laughed again, louder this time and looked over at me looking at him.

"You really wrote this?" he asked.

I nodded.

"Damn," he said. "You're really good. Don't even bother finishing mine."

I smiled and turned back to his page, hoping the flush on my face wasn't as obvious as it felt.

His was also a comedy and very funny, though a little disjointed in the set ups. It read as though he was too eager to get to the bit and unwilling to put in the time to set up the joke properly. He was still like that. Or was. His whole life was spent being too eager to get where he wanted to go.

"You're a really good writer," he said as he passed the pages back. "Is that what you want to do? Screenwriting?"

"No. I mean, I guess I do want to write, but my goal is directing. I'd love to write and direct."

"Sweet. Me too. Well, more the directing part. I may need you to teach me how to write like that."

"That's nice. Thanks."

"I'm Jace," he said in my direction.

I knew.

"Jonathan. Or Johnny."

"Well, Jonathan or Johnny, your work is great. Quick to establish your characters and very funny delivery. I get what you're saying and where you're going."

"Thanks."

"What about mine?"

"Oh," I started, looking down at the pages, "I'm not done yet."

He raised his eyebrows and held both hands up, giving me the space to finish. I was suddenly conscious of his eyes on me as I looked at his page. Focusing every ounce of mental strength I had, I looked down at his words and continued reading.

"It's really good," I said when I finished and handed it back.

"Oh stop it," he teased before cupping his chin with his hand, leaning over in my direction. "Tell me more."

We moved easily from the assignment to movies we liked, directors we wanted to emulate and hopes and dreams for our own creative futures. Talking to Jace was like learning how to talk for the first time. When he spoke words, they had new meanings. Nothing else was happening in the world; it was just him talking to you like you were the most important thing in his orbit.

The professor began his lecture on hooks and we cut our conversation to listen. Once the class was over, we resumed the conversation again and walked slowly down the hall together, right where we had left off. And it was like that. One long, never-ending conversation between us. We hadn't stopped talking until now.

"He talked all the goddamn time," Dick said in exasperation, though I didn't believe it.

"You liked it," I said, still watching the ceiling. "You miss it."

"No shit," Dick said, laughing Jace's laugh, "That's why we're still here, talking to each other, day after day after day— now I never have to leave you. I told you I'd find you. Remember that?"

I did.

"Come on," I said, tugging on my backpack. "We've got to finish this assignment."

"Jesus, Johnny, do you always do what you're told?" He moved out of the way of a kid rolling by on his skateboard.

I looked at him like I wasn't sure if he was joking. "I do when it can change my grade in a class."

"You're acing all your classes and you know it. It'd be impossible for you to fail anything."

He pulled out a pack of cigarettes and offered me one. I shook my head.

"You don't smoke?"

"Never have."

"Just try it."

He could sense my skepticism. I was beginning to think

making people do things they hadn't done before was one of Jace's favorite pastimes.

"Why?"

"Don't you want to live a life knowing what things feel like? I don't want to ever be able to say I've never done x, y, or z."

"That's dumb," I started and laughed as his face turned into a scowl. "There's a lot of things you shouldn't do that you haven't done before. Do you want to know what it tastes like to drink bleach?"

"Now *you're* being dumb."

I took the cigarette. "Don't make fun of me for it."

"Why would I make fun of you? I'd never make fun of someone trying something new. Someone who dares to be alive. Isn't that the point of life? To live the most? What's dumb about that?"

I grinned. His philosophical bullshit always got me.

"You're a fucking writer. Your whole existence should be experiencing every little piece of life you can. How can you expect anyone to believe your words if you don't believe them yourself? Here," he offered, extending his hand as we started walking. He pulled out his lighter from his back pocket and lit the cigarette before handing it back to me.

Dropping my backpack by our tree, I sat before sticking the cigarette in my mouth. I inhaled cautiously and sputtered a cough before turning to him. He was grinning from ear to ear.

"I'm really proud of you, Johnny. You've now gained another human experience."

"It's not a great one," I said, scrunching my face in concern and feeling the pressure at the back of my nose.

He sat next to me and laughed his loud, obnoxious laugh. I stuck the cigarette between my lips and tried it again. It was better this time and didn't make me choke.

Reaching over, he gently pulled it from my mouth and took a drag. "Nap time. Are you reading?"

I nodded and pulled my book from my backpack.

"Wake me up when you're done."

He laid back on the ground with his arms wrapped behind his head and closed his eyes. The cigarette perched between his lips had a little wisp of smoke trailing from it and he was the sexiest person I'd ever seen in my entire life, I was sure of it.

"Do you think we'd be friends if we met somewhere else?" I asked, leaning against my knee, pulled up to my chest. Part of me guessed that Jace and I would have never been friends if we hadn't met in the way we did. The other part of me doubted if we *were* ever actually friends.

"Of course," he reassured, the cigarette bobbing up and down as he spoke. "In fact, I bet in every dimension or universe, there's versions of us, finding each other and creating some cool shit. I think no matter what, we find each other. Don't you think?"

I smiled at him, knowing he couldn't see it. "That's nice to think about."

"Well, I'll look for you if you look for me. Deal?"

"Deal."

He stuck out his hand, eyes still closed, with pinky extended to make a commitment. I leaned forward toward him and gripped his pinky with mine. He shook it vigorously, his body shaking in silent laughter as he did. When he let go, he reached up and pulled out the cigarette.

"Now let me get some sleep. Wake me up when you're done, nerd."

The shadow of the swirling fan in my bedroom fell upon his face and I could hear the little motor running over and over. I listened to the quiet swish and I rolled to pull out my phone from my back pocket. The call to Riley had to be first.

"What are you doing?" Dick asked, army crawling inch by inch to my face. "Are you having second thoughts about what a piece of shit you are?"

"Would you shut the fuck up?"

"Johnny?" she asked, concerned. "Are you okay? Who are you talking to?"

"Hey," I started, realizing I didn't know what I was going to say.

"What's wrong?"

"Yeah, no, nothing, I need to talk to you. Can I come over?"

"Of course. I'm on my way home now. Meet in like forty-five minutes?"

"Great. See you in a bit."

I hung up the phone and felt so heavy I didn't know if I'd be able to get up. What was I going to say to her? How could I make this make sense? I would have to change clothes first.

"What are you going to say?" Dick asked, now on the floor next to me, his wings behind his head as we looked up at the ceiling together.

"I don't know."

"You should tell her that her life is a lie. That Jace was a monster and she lucked out by having him kill himself."

"I'm not going to say that."

"Promise?" he asked, sticking out a singular wing feather.

The pit of unease was growing as I reached over and accepted the feather, shaking it slowly.

8

SEASON 1 - EPISODE 8
MacGuffin

"Are you sure you're okay?" Riley asked when she answered the door and saw my face.

I felt like I was about to throw up.

"Johnny, you're scaring me." She looked down to the box in my hand. "What is that?"

"All of Jace's stuff from his office, on his desk. I figured you'd want it."

"Oh, thanks. Can you stick it in his office? I don't want to deal with it right now. Is that all?" She stepped aside so I could come in.

"Sure," I offered, unsure how to transition to the envelope sitting on top.

I headed back to Jace's office and she followed me, trying to look inside as we walked.

"What all is in it?" she asked, as I put in on the desk.

She poked around and pulled out a picture of her and Jace's wedding. Her face remained blank at the memory and the pit in my stomach grew.

"Do you remember the pastor at the wedding?"

I nodded. "Yeah, I do. That was wild."

"So many things like that have been in my mind lately. Has that happened to you? Big moments and the little ones. Like watching a reel of Jace's life or something."

"Yeah," I admitted. "I know what you mean."

"What's this?" she asked, reaching for the envelope.

I took it from her before she could get it. "We need to sit."

Her face fell as she moved back and sat in the leather chair against the wall. I pulled out the chair from Jace's desk and sat before thinking maybe I shouldn't. I looked at her briefly to try and determine if she took it as some kind of overstep, but her face revealed nothing.

"This is from a lawyer," I started, leaning forward to hand it over. "It's alleging that Dick is an infringement on someone else's idea. That Dick isn't Jace's original creation."

She took the envelope and pulled the paper out, reading the words over and over. I watched her lips move silently as she read the condemnation the letter contained. When she finished, she looked up at me.

"I need a minute."

She hurried out of the room and I wasn't sure what to do. I thought for a brief minute that maybe I had to follow her, but guessed if she asked for space I was supposed to respect that.

Instead, I looked down at the desk, where Jace's notes and papers littered the space. It was as unkempt as his production office desk and my fingers traced over the ideas. There were a few little animated Dicks as well as Mr. Bramblebutt, the little scrappy dog Jace had been incredibly proud of.

One of the sticky notes caught my attention when I saw my name:

Johnny wants to redeem Dick—don't let him.

My eyebrows fell as I read it. It was something we had fought about weeks before he died. Season 1 was all introductions and Season 2 was audience buy-in. But Season 3 had to offer some small glimpse of redemption for Dick. It had to. Sometimes I questioned whether or not Jace understood the idea of story. A good story had to include simple elements— conflict, journey, resolution. It could subvert those expectations to a degree; without their existence, there was no growth. But growth had never been Jace's strength. Jace firmly believed that every episode had to end in the same place it began—Dick never aged and never learned.

I glanced back down to Jace's notes. I picked up the paper and underneath in neat little lines was the phrase *no redemption* written over and over and over on the note below.

"Should have been a clue," I mumbled.

I began to wonder for the first time since receiving the information I had, whether this legal issue was the reason he killed himself. I wondered why he hadn't just told me. He should have known that no matter what it was, we could have faced it, together. That we could have gotten out of this alive. Surely he knew that.

He never hid things from me. At least I didn't think he did. Obviously, now, in the wake of this, I had to wonder.

"Did you know?" Riley asked from behind me as she re-entered the room.

She was holding a different envelope between two glasses and a bottle of whiskey.

"What's this?" I asked, turning back toward her as she sat.

"I need a drink," she said flatly as she poured a little in both glasses.

"What's the other envelope?" I asked, suddenly more worried than before.

She ignored my question and pushed one of the glasses in my direction before she grabbed her own and raised it. I picked it up and listened to the sound of the glass clinking together as they touched.

"To making it out of this alive," she offered.

"To surviving."

I took a sip of the amber liquid and put it back down on the desk.

"We'll get to this in a minute. First, let's back up. Did you know?"

My eyes returned to Jace's pages, *don't let him,* unsure of how to answer. "About which part?"

"The lawsuit."

"No."

"Then what part did you know?"

"I mean, I was there, in college. I think I kind of always thought something was weird, but I didn't really know."

"Tell me."

"I don't know," I hesitated.

She moved across the room and dragged one of the other chairs from the side of the room to sit right next to me.

"Johnny," she started, reaching out to touch my arm. "I need to know this."

I highly doubted that.

"Will it help?"

She laughed but there was no humor in it. "I question everything now. I can't see a single memory from this house without questioning it all. In fact, it's really kind of bullshit that you kept this from me all these years."

I sighed.

"Like what the fuck? What else are you keeping from me?"

She really didn't want to open that door.

"Some of it wasn't mine to share."

"What does that even mean? How can something like that not be something that I would want to know about? How much were you two keeping from me?"

I didn't know how to answer her. Was it really my place to tell her all of Jace's shit? It wasn't on me to explain to her who she married.

"You know what it makes me feel like? If I'm being really honest?"

"What?" I asked, finally turning to look at her.

"It feels like you two had a secret little thing I wasn't allowed in on. And I feel like I tried really hard ever since I met you, to set boundaries that I was in a relationship with Jace and I knew you were too, in your own way. I respected that. And you respected us. Right?"

I nodded.

"But finding out you guys had your own secrets is weird to me and I don't know what to do with that. I'm still mad at Jace and I don't want to be mad at you, but I don't know how to handle this. Okay?"

Her voice started shaking and tears forming in her large eyes. Slowly, I reached over and took her hand. She didn't pull back and little by little her fingers moved to close over mine. I didn't know how to define my relationship with Jace and sure didn't know how to define my relationship with Riley.

"I wasn't trying to keep things from you. I really felt like it wasn't my place to talk about things before you and Jace got together."

"Tell me about Dick."

"It's true we came up with Dick in college, but there's more to it than that."

I let go of her hand and leaned back to try and clear the

decades of fog that was clouding my brain. I hadn't thought about it in a long time.

"Dick started out as an otter," I said, and Riley laughed.

"What?" she asked.

"Yeah, I don't know. That was my idea. I don't know where it came from, honestly, but he was an otter and I don't remember if his name was Dick. He was a detective though. Jace did draw a few prototypes. I'm sure he destroyed all of that."

She shook her head. "No, actually, I have one of his drawings of an otter. I had no idea that's what it was."

"Well, you will either need to keep it or burn it by the end of this."

Her smile fell. "Go on."

"We had done this other thing for a class. A buddy cop thing. It was humans, not animals. And I think I always kind of assumed that the Dick idea sprung from the merging of the otter and buddy cop drama. It made sense in my mind. I do remember the night that Jace showed me Dick in the form he is now.

"We were in the dorms then and I had come back late one night, and he was drawing, which wasn't that uncommon. As lazy as he is—" I cut myself off. "Jesus. I'm sorry. Was. As lazy as he was lately, he was the total opposite in college if you can believe it. He drew all the time. Little comics and cartoons of our professors, that kind of thing."

Riley leaned forward with a smile, remembering that version of Jace.

"But he was so excited when I got there and pushed a piece of paper in front of my face. It was Dick. In his little coat. The words were carefully placed above him in the font we ended up actually using for the show. There was something about putting that original piece into life that we both were absolutely obsessed with. Like seeing something go from your imagination into real space and time was a high we endlessly chased."

"So what happened?"

"I told him I loved it."

That was true. I loved Dick the moment I saw him. It made more sense than the otter. It was a better bit—Dick the dick, who was also a dick. Jace had a knack for taking an idea and making it what it was supposed to be. He didn't care about what Dick became or stood for or represented to others. It was a joke and one that he would always find funny.

I did add the fedora. That was my one contribution to the way that Dick was presented. When I saw him, I knew he had to have a little hat. Jace fought with me on the hat because of how difficult it could be to animate the hat as he moved, but conceded when we agreed that the hat would remain on Dick's head no matter what, more like hair than a separate piece.

That rule realistically lasted half of the first season. Once Jace was out of the mainstream animation process, he didn't really give a shit what did or didn't make it harder to draw.

He ended up trading the fedora for a variety of different outfits. I often found myself writing the scenarios of the show around what kind of outfits I could imagine Dick finding himself wearing.

"So, what happened?" Riley asked, pulling me back to the present.

"A few days later, I saw Jace and another kid, Hansome, in a fight in the cafeteria."

"Handsome?" Riley interrupted. "The kid's name is Handsome?"

I chuckled. "No d. Han-some. I don't know where on earth he got it. It's probably not his real name. I never asked. I would guess that's who is involved in this, though the letter doesn't mention the client's name."

Riley startled suddenly in her seat so quickly it made me jump. She reached down and grabbed the envelope that she had brought in. It was from the same lawyer.

"What is it?"

"I think it's a summons. I hadn't opened it."

"What?"

She handed it over to me. "Honestly, I was going to give it to Bruce. It never occurred to me that something bad was in it. You know how many of those lawsuit things we get. I assumed this was no different and I had no energy to deal with any of it."

I slid my fingers under the seal and once opened, I pulled the top paper out. It was a summons. On the defendant's side, I saw the name, clear as day: Hansome Hill.

"Hill," I said in realization, showing her the paper. "Hansome Hill."

"I refuse to believe that's his real name," she said, reaching over to get another drink. It had been so long since I had thought about him. He was relatively handsome—or was at the time. He was a trust fund baby, that much I did know.

"Hansome was an art major and spent all the time we had together in class reminding everyone how brave he was for defying his family expectations and going into the arts, despite his father's business acumen. His dad was some kind of Wall Street executive or something. A lot of us in college tried to outdo each other on how hard we had it and it was always difficult for Hansome to compete with some of us." *Especially someone like Jace who had an alcoholic piece of shit father*, I wanted to add.

"You saw Hansome and Jace in a fight?" Riley asked.

"Yeah, I don't really remember what happened. But we were eating and Hansome like dramatically challenged Jace to some kind of fight across the room. It was like a movie scene, which I knew Jace must have loved. They moved toward one another slowly, from opposite sides of the room. Once Jace found out what they were actually fighting about, he pulled Hansome outside. That's how I knew it must have been something, because Jace would have never given up the opportunity to make a scene, unless he knew he would come out on the wrong end of it."

"True."

"Jace came back in the room later and acted like nothing happened."

"Did you ask him about it?"

I nodded, emptying my glass. "Sure, but he shrugged it off. I feel like he eventually told me it was over a girl they were both dating or something. I don't really remember all of that part."

Riley nodded as she processed the new information. "But you did find out later? Or how did you know?"

"Yeah. Much later."

"What happened?"

FLASHBACK SEQUENCE TOLD AS A VOICE OVER TO RILEY

It was when we were moving. When he moved in here, actually. Jace bought this house when we were living together. After you guys started dating. When it was time to move out of the apartment we were in, I was helping him pack his stuff up because he moved out a few months before I did.

His room was a mess, which shouldn't surprise you. He had piles of paper and art everywhere. This was right before we started *Scraping By* and he had drafts and drafts of scripts everywhere on the floor. He claims I wrote that, but really he did a lot of the rewrites on it. Anyways, I'm getting distracted.

In one of the piles I was going through, there was one drawing that stuck out.

"What the fuck is this?" I asked as I held up the drawing.

"It looks like a shitty early drawing of Dick," Jace replied, defiantly.

"This isn't your work."

"How do you know?" he asked, barely acknowledging me from the other side of the floor.

"All I ever do is look at your art, dipshit. I can tell you didn't draw this. What is it?"

My curiosity was starting to overtake me and his reluctance to be honest about it was starting to make me uncomfortable, though I didn't really know why. Jace didn't really *lie* a lot, but he was pretty good at withholding information that was vital to understanding what the full situation was. I don't know if I can be that honest, but you know it's true.

"It's a dumb drawing, Jesus, move on. We've still got two more boxes to go through."

The funny thing was, I almost did. I almost put the paper down and it would have just been a piece of another piece in his archive of Dick that lived in your closet. But I noticed a signature. Jace never signed his doodles, he said it was too egotistical, even for him. Yeah, I know. But I knew the signature the minute I saw it clearer.

"Hansome."

Jace stopped digging and looked up as though debating whether or not he could get out of it. The longer he waited, the less likely I was to believe anything that was about to come out of his mouth.

"Jason," I said quietly, "tell me exactly where you got this drawing."

"You're right. I got it from Hansome."

"But it's Dick."

"It isn't."

"Jason. I need you to tell me exactly why you have this."

He claimed he bought the rights from Hansome. He said he saw the drawing and knew that our Dick shouldn't be an otter and this was the version he had been searching for. It was the strike of inspiration he had been waiting to be hit with. He told me then that he paid Hansome for the image. I asked if he paid him after the fight in the cafeteria and he wouldn't say yes or no. I think I believed he did at the time. I honestly now don't know if he did or not. If he did, I don't think Hansome would be doing what he's doing now?

END OF FLASHBACK

"But why now?" Riley asked. "Like after all these years, why is he suing now?"

"I don't know. Maybe the popularity of the show? Like he knows Jace has actually made money off it?"

Riley sighed a heavy sigh and poured another knuckle. She raised the bottle in my direction and I pushed my glass forward. She filled it before putting the bottle down.

"So what now?" I asked.

Riley took a sip of her whiskey as though thinking carefully about her response. There was silence until she set it down, the ring of the glass against the desk echoing in the room.

"I don't know. Is that all you've been keeping from me?"

I considered my words, unsure how to move forward. "I wasn't keeping that from you, really, I had no idea that it was something that needed to be addressed. I didn't keep things from you or Jace. I never wanted us to change, but I also never wanted to lose Jace. And since I have, nothing's made sense anymore. All of this keeps getting worse and worse and I'm sorry for that."

"Yeah," she agreed after a moment. "I know. Me too."

"Are you mad at me?"

"I don't know."

I appreciated her honesty.

"Can I ask you something really personal? I just need to know."

A hollow pit started in my chest as I prepared myself for her question. I had a guess as to what it was.

"Did you and Jace..." she trailed off.

I wasn't going to finish the sentence for her.

"Did we what?"

She chewed on her bottom lip before looking me directly in the eyes. "Did you ever hook up?"

"No."

She nodded slowly.

"Jace wasn't into men," I said quietly, letting the questions rest in the space between us.

She kept nodding. "Why did you protect him so much?"

I shrugged, unsure if I could explain to her. "He needed it sometimes and I needed it sometimes. I know people saw Jace's asshole side. But sometimes, he was the only person there for me. And we, I don't know, got each other. In a way no one else did. Once you create something that you care so much about, you're kind of stuck with that person. Like a fucked up kind of joint-custody or something."

"Did you guys not trust me or what?"

I laughed and instantly regretted it after seeing the genuine hurt in her eyes.

"I trust you more than anyone I know. I thought we knew each other more than friends, or something, you know? I really feel like you and Jace were my family."

It wasn't a lie. I did see Riley as my family. And I think by now she knew that Jace occupied a version of that space that likely veered into other territory but we didn't have to talk about that.

"I didn't... don't..." she stopped herself, pulling her braids back and tying them in a high ponytail distractedly. "I feel like I'm stuck, Johnny. I need help."

"With what?"

"I knew who Jace was when I married him. I know that. I took the bad with the good. And it's been hard the last few years. I have, I don't know, guilt, I guess, that there are some days lately I don't think about him at all. It has been so easy being on my own sometimes. And then other times, I wake up on the bathroom floor because I've finally just passed out from exhaustion. I want to make sense of this—of him—and of you and find a way to deal with what we've lost. I don't know anymore. I don't know what I'm even supposed to be doing. And learning this, now, it makes me question a lot. You know?"

I did know. I leaned back in my chair, trying to take in all she was saying. I was processing the same emotions and didn't know if I was the best person to offer any advice. Stretching my arm, I grabbed my glass and emptied it in one gulp.

There *was* one other thing I hadn't told Riley. I didn't know if Jace had ever told her or not, but I guessed with what I was learning that there were more things he kept from her than not. I fully believed that Jace had attempted suicide before.

———

The library was supposed to be a quiet place, but all around me students chatted without a care in the world as to who might be near them actually trying to study for a general anatomy final.

"Johnny?" I heard a voice call from a table over.

I looked up to see Kristin Meyers grabbing her books to move to where I was. "Can I join you?"

My finger rested on a paragraph about femurs and I forced a smile. "Sure."

"What are you doing here so late?"

"Studying," I admitted, tapping my finger along the textbook page. "Aren't you?"

"I'm supposed to be working on a paper, but you know, senioritis."

"Yeah."

I looked back down at the book and she opened her laptop to resume her work. "What are you doing after graduation?"

"Not sure yet," I said, flipping the page. "I'm waiting to hear back on this internship with a studio. What about you?"

"I've been doing some PA work at Bad Robot. I'll keep doing that for a while."

"Nice."

"What about Jace? What is he doing?"

"I don't know," I said absentmindedly. "You'd have to ask him."

She was quiet and I looked up from my book to see what the problem was. "What's the situation with him and Sarah Loren?"

"I don't know," I repeated. "You'd have to ask him."

Grinning, she nodded. Satisfied with her answer, she turned back to her laptop. "What about you? Are you dating anyone?"

"No."

"My roommate is single. She's super cute. I can give her your number if you want?"

"Oh," I said, looking up. "No, sorry, I'm gay, actually. Thank you, though."

"Oh my god, I'm sorry," she said, her face flushing. "That was dumb of me to assume."

"Not really," I said in an attempt to reassure her. "It's kind of the default."

"Geez, Johnny, I'm really sorry."

"Nothing to be sorry about," I said with a smile, pushing at the corner of the pages in my book.

My cell phone started ringing in my pocket and I pulled it out to look. It was an L.A. number.

I flipped the top open. "Hello?"

"Jonathan Goodwin?"

"Yeah?"

"I'm Susan, a nurse at Cedars Sinai Medical Center. We've got a patient here, Jason Van Noy. He gave you as his emergency contact."

"What happened? Is he okay?"

I stood as Susan kept talking and I was trying to focus on what she was saying but also on getting all of my things together. *Fall,* I heard, and *broken wrist.*

"What? Is he okay?"

"Yes, he's doing alright, but we wanted to contact you. The doctor actually would like to speak with you. Would you have some time to talk to him?"

"Yeah, I can come see Jace now. Would that work?"

"Stop by the front desk when you get here."

I hung up and realized I didn't have a car. "Hey, I'm sorry to bother you, but do you know anyone with a car?"

"I do. What's wrong with Jace?" Kristin said, also starting to collect her things.

"I don't know—he was in some accident. Can you take me Cedars?"

"Yeah, let's go."

I followed Kristin in silence, hoping she wasn't feeling chatty and trying to recall all the words the nurse said on the phone. It didn't make sense that the doctor would want to talk to me. I didn't even know I was his emergency contact.

We got to the hospital and Kristin dropped me off at the emergency room before going to park the car. At the front desk, one of the nurses called someone before telling me Jace's room number.

"Can you wait over there for a minute, Mr. Goodwin?"

"Sure," I said, folding my arms across my chest.

After a few moments, a man entered the lobby area wearing a white coat. He started to walk to me and I met him near the door. "Doctor?"

"Doctor Gardner. I wanted to have a quick chat about Jason Van Noy. Does Jason suffer from any mental illness that you know of? Depression? Bipolar Disorder?"

I guessed it wasn't the time to joke about Jace's whole life being one giant mental illness. "I don't know. He can be depressed sometimes, I guess? Why?"

"We found some medication on him. And he took quite a lot of it. It's a drug that's commonly used for intentional overdosing. Has he ever attempted suicide before?"

"Not that I know of," I said, shocked.

"He's pretty adamant that this was an accident and not intentional. But as his emergency contact, I feel like you should be aware. We're keeping him for twenty-four hours for observation. If we have reason to believe he will be a danger to himself, I'll have to have him transported to a facility."

"Sure." My hands were starting to feel numb. "Can I see him?"

"Of course. I'd like to keep that information between us, if you don't mind, for now. Just until we can sort things out."

"Right."

"The front desk will give you the directions." He pulled out a card. "Please give me a call if anything else comes up."

"Sure. Thanks."

The doctor disappeared back behind the doors and I wasn't sure I would be able to face Jace directly. Surely this was all some kind of misunderstanding.

I made my way into the room. Jace was in the bed, covered up to his shoulders with his injured arm resting on top of a pillow. His entire hand was wrapped in a cast.

"What the hell, Jace. Are you okay?"

He smiled when I walked in, and I could tell by his heavy lids that he was sedated.

"Johnny," he said, his voice cracking.

"What happened?"

"I fell. Stupid accident."

"Fell?" I asked, pulling a chair close to the bed. "Fell where?"

"Out walking. One of the canyon trails."

You were out walking? On a trail? And fell? By accident?" I emphasized each phrase as a question.

He looked at me and nodded. "Yeah. I fell."

"I want to be clear that I'm understanding what you're saying. You, Jason Van Noy, who doesn't do physical exercise unless something is chasing him, was out walking along the canyon trail and fell, completely on accident."

"What are you saying?" he asked, narrowing his eyes from the bed.

I shook my head as my mouth drew into a little line. I wasn't supposed to push it.

"It's just hard to believe, I guess."

"Stupid is what you mean," he said, letting his head fall to the side.

Kristin appeared at the door to the room and I had forgotten she was even involved.

"Jason?" she asked, moving forward.

"Who are you?" he asked, groggy.

"Kristin gave me a ride," I offered.

"Hi, Kristin." Jace looked from me to Kristin before closing his eyes. I pulled the chair closer and settled in, prepared to stay all night with him if I had to.

"Do you need anything?" Kristin asked, looking from me to Jace.

"No," I said. "Thank you so much for the ride, but I'll stay here for now."

"Here, let me get your number and I can come get you when they release him?"

I complied and settled back into the chair, trying to get comfortable. I assumed Jace had fallen asleep, but once Kristin left, he stirred slightly.

"Sorry, man," he said quietly. "You're a good friend."

"Yeah," I replied, unsure what else to say.

He reached with his good hand and stretched his arm toward me, eyes still closed. I took his hand and held it gently in my own. "Get some sleep."

A deep silence settled in the room around us and I let my head fall against the edge of the chair as I watched him, still cradling his hand in mine. I wasn't sure what to do. I didn't think of Jace as being depressed in that sense. Like, not suicidal. But how did I know what suicidal really looked like?

It was possible it was an accident. He was doing stupid shit all the time. He looked peaceful as he slept, his wavy hair pushed against the base of his neck. What did it mean that he lived a life where suicide was indistinguishable from his day-to-day bullshit?

If he was telling me it was an accident, then I had to believe that it was just an accident. Was I supposed to tell Riley now? That it was something we had gone through before?

There was a statistic I read later about suicide attempts. Something like forty percent of people who fail one attempt will attempt another or something. I don't remember exactly. But I always wondered, in the back of my mind, about Jace from then on. He had adamantly denied it was intentional. He stuck to the story that he was simply out walking and fucked up. I didn't know then, but I guess I know now.

He was too much sometimes. It was always too much. Too happy, too sad. Everything had to be the biggest or the best. It exhausted me; I can't imagine how it must have twisted him.

I think part of that was why, no matter what others said about him, and no matter what he said about me, I couldn't help but feel the need to protect him—from himself more than anyone. We were both incredibly broken in our own ways, but allowing each other to take care of the other let us ignore our own brokenness. It was textbook codependency, I guessed.

"Were you happy?" I asked Riley.

"Sometimes," she said, raising her eyebrows high as though surprising herself at her answer. "I don't believe in like, this pursuit of happiness in life though. Like sometimes you're happy and sometimes you aren't. I know when I'm not happy that I will be happy again, eventually, and vice versa. I do know I was never responsible for Jace being happy or unhappy though. You can't put that on another person. And Jace was often either really happy or really unhappy."

I nodded. That was definitely true. It was always in extremes.

"Were you happy?" she asked me.

"Yeah," I admitted. "I was. Getting the chance to make something like *Dick* was all I had ever wanted. And I am glad I got the chance to do it with Jace."

She looked down at the ground. "There were times where I really hated you, Johnny."

"What?" I asked, surprised.

"Yeah, if I'm being really honest here. There was space Jace held for you in his life that I could never reach and I hated it. And now, I think, maybe, I feel like it makes sense why? You really were his person, more than I ever could have been. And I think I knew that, obviously, but now, it seems like, I don't know..."

"What do you mean?" I asked. "Because of Hansome?"

"Not that." She got up and left the room again. She was gone a few minutes before she came back and plopped a notebook down on the desk. "You can keep that."

My confusion deepened as I looked down at the notebook. I hadn't seen it before. Jace wasn't one to keep a notebook with him. As I flipped open the cover, it was definitely his handwriting inside.

It was pages and pages of his thoughts and ideas. I wasn't sure what any of it had to do with me.

"Just take it. I'm exhausted and need to go to bed. I know we'll talk later."

"Hold on. I'm so confused. What is this and why do I feel like I'm in trouble for something?"

"I'm sorry, I really need some space right now. I'll give all this to Bruce and he'll probably reach out to you. You're not listed on this, but you own *Dick*, so you probably want to be involved."

"Sure," I said, standing up, still slightly confused. I slid the notebook under my arm and headed for the door.

"Are you okay to drive?" she asked behind me.

"Yeah."

"Thanks for the box," she said quickly before turning away.

Once outside, I stood in the cool air for a moment before heading for my car. I drove home in silence, doing my best to ignore the notebook sitting on the empty seat next to me. As soon as I opened the door, I heard the familiar voice of Dick filling my house.

"Why didn't you read it? Aren't you dying to know what it says?"

"I don't know."

"Read it," he demanded, hopping up the stairs one at a time as I walked.

"Isn't it better to let the dead stay dead?"

Dick laughed. "You're asking me? I'm the literal personification of not letting the dead stay dead. You're not very good at that, if you haven't noticed."

I tossed the notebook on the bed and went to the bathroom to get ready to sleep. When I walked back in the room I checked briefly to make sure the notebook was still there. I pulled out my phone and put in on the charger and my eyes wandered back to the object that was starting to consume all my thoughts.

Slowly, I reached over to see what all the fuss was about and opened the notebook to the first page.

9

I Have Something to Tell You...Never Mind...

My therapist says I should start writing my thoughts in a notebook to a) keep them straight and b) look back on all the progress I've made next year. I told him that a) I don't need a fucking notebook and b) I plan on making no progress. So, there's that.

DICK

DUCK

FICK

FUCK

I'm supposed to figure out my triggers. Things that trigger me:

- *Idiots*
- *Dealing with idiots*

- *Listening to people chew*
- *Listening to idiots chew*
- *The inevitable void of being abandoned by everyone I know.*

I'm jealous sometimes of seeing people in love. I honestly don't even know if I know what that feels like. I love Riley, I know I do, but like it just doesn't feel the way I guess I thought it would feel. Honestly, I don't feel anything most of the time. My therapist says that's due to "mental illness" but what the fuck does he know.

I think I'm most jealous when I see how easy it is for Johnny to love those around him. It comes so easily to him. His heart's too big for his own good. He lets people use and abuse him. He lets me use and abuse him and I don't know why.

I mean, I do know why, because he's in love with me and that makes me feel even more like shit. He'd be better off without me. He'd finally let go of me and find someone who can love him the way he deserves. Doesn't that mean I love him in some way? Surely it does, somehow.

I want him and Riley to be happy. I want them to be better than they are now. I want to just not be a problem in their lives.

I wake up every day and don't want to be here any more. I wish I could explain it to them.

I don't know.

What the fuck do I know.

Maybe the therapist is right.

Fuck him.

Fuck this.

**Don't forget to ask Johnny about Taylor.*

N A M E S:

ANNA WHITLOW
JOSHUA JAMES
CHRISTOPHER ELBOW
TYLER SAYRE
CIERA HENDERSON
DEEDEE TRUITT
JES M.

Degrees of relation to known sources.

I'm supposed to try to be healthy. Dr. Dickfuck thinks I can improve my overall mental health if I eat real food instead of junk and alcohol, but I think Dr. Dickfuck has never had sex once in his life.

Things I Ate Today:

- *Donut – not healthy*
- *Banana – super healthy*
- *Pizza – not that unhealthy*
- *Beer – maybe unhealthy*
- *Roasted vegetables – the most healthy*
- *Chicken?*
- *Rolls – don't even care*
- *More beer – slightly less healthy*
- *Candy bar – the least healthy*

Things I Watched Johnny Look at Instead of Eating

- *My donut*
- *My pizza*
- ***he drank the beer***

- *Whatever shit salad he had for dinner*

I don't know why I need to write my triggers when he's literally a walking eating disorder.

He's my trigger. Him avoiding the shit in his life triggers me. He can't even look at himself in a mirror. What the hell is that? What the hell does he see when he sees himself and why? What is that?

Maybe that's why we're so close. We look at ourselves and hate what we see but we look at the other and love every bit of it. How fucked up is that?

I think Riley's going to leave me. I don't know how she lasted this long. In therapy today we talked about abandonment. Or specifically how I have issues with it. Dr. Dickfuck says that I create scenarios to protect myself in case people leave when really whether or not they leave is out of my control. But it's not all out of my control. If Riley leaves it will be because of something I did. But also, she should leave. I want her to leave. That's dumb, I don't want her to leave. I don't know what I'd do without her.

Fucking Johnny. Johnny would never leave me. I'll leave him before he leaves me. We're stuck together. Not to be gay or whatever, but I think I could handle Riley leaving me better than I could Johnny.

I don't know, this is fucking stupid. How is this helping anything? I still feel numb in the world around me. This isn't helping me at all. Fuck you, Dr. Dickfuck.

I D E A S: Cheeseburger factory, Broadway backstage crew fights, whales? Fake racecar driver.

<u>*Pay your fucking parking ticket you dipshit*</u>

My homework today is to think of all the things that make me happy. Feeling the sun on my face. Feeling the ocean against my skin. Finishing a piece. Working with Johnny. Cooking a really good steak. Being right. Being right when Johnny is wrong—the absolute best. The first sip of whiskey. The last sip of whiskey. Sleeping in. Finding the

Dr. Dickfuck thinks I should explore writing poetry because I'm apparently no good at long form feeling telling. I reminded him I was nominated for an Emmy for my exact skills of long form feeling telling. Here's my poem:

In spite of everything
I still want to kill myself.
Dr. Dickfuck, you suck at your job.
Dr. Dickfuck, you suck balls.
When I'm dead, you'll feel bad
And still, I'll feel nothing at all.
So brave.

(I know this isn't a work notebook, but this is all I have in my hands and I have to remind myself to tell Johnny that Mercury called about the interview—I think it should be at Dilly's. Ok—I can actually text Johnny right now. I'm going to text him. That makes more sense)

If I sit too long, I start thinking about systems and it scares me. Everything in the world was created by someone else with some other idea. For power or survival or both. But none of it means anything. We're here, we survive as long as we can, and then we die. It's systems of things and patterns. Barcodes on piles of shit that will sit in a landfill once we've consumed and consumed. Like a disease. We use everything we touch. Systems created to cover our secrets and make us feel better. We buy more to bury the void of existence. And it only works until we need more money. And we make more to buy more and buy more to feel more. Does it work? Does it really still work like that? I don't know.

OK—I'm abandoning this. I'm done with this and done with therapy—tried it, it didn't take. I'm wasting time here.

End Scene. Exit Jason.

I flipped through the notebook, desperately searching for more sacred text, more clues or insight into the very real and honest Jason Van Noy. But it was page after page of blank nothingness —empty space of an unfinished life.

10

My phone buzzed on the bed next to me and I pulled my eyes from the notebook to the phone. Barbara.

I answered it on speaker, looking back at the notebook. "What's up?"

"I have two things set up for you. Can you meet Lee Young tomorrow at three? And Wiley afterwards at the studio around five?"

"Sure."

"Okay, great, that's great. What's wrong? You sound weird," Barbara said, her voice jumping up and down in intonation.

"I just said 'sure'."

"But you said it weird."

"No, that's my normal voice. Thank you, Barbara. I'll be there for both. Can you text me the information?" I asked.

"Sure," she replied, over-emphasizing the word.

"Great. Thank you." I hung up before she could ask any more questions.

My fingers slid back to the notebook. "What's a cheeseburger factory?"

"Maybe it's a factory where burgers are the workers. And they make cows," Dick replied on his back in the middle of the bed.

"That's gross."

"Or cows make burgers?"

"Sick."

"Or burgers make burgers?"

"Okay."

"Well something has to be making something at a factory," he demanded.

I looked at Dick stretched out with his wings folded behind his head. He reminded me of Jace.

"I guess we'll never know," I responded and slid next to him on the bed, holding up the notebook to re-read it.

"Just imagine if he had said some of that stuff to your face. He might still be alive."

"Dick," I mumbled, trying to tune him out as my eyes scanned the pages once more. *We look at ourselves and hate what we see but we look at the other and love every bit of it.* He wasn't wrong. I guess I had never really thought he was serious about hating himself. He really hated himself enough to give up.

I would have done anything to get him to see himself the way I saw him. Did that mean he felt the same about me?

"Don't like that," I announced, tossing the book to the floor.

"We could burn it tomorrow," Dick said, snuggling into the sheets before I turned off the lights.

"Yeah," I agreed. "Maybe tomorrow, we burn it."

I climbed in bed and stared at the ceiling, afraid my brain would keep me from sleeping once again, but instead found myself drifting instantly.

When I woke to the loud sound of an alarm I didn't remember setting, I noticed the sun streaming through the curtains I didn't close the night before and got up. When I stepped out of bed, my foot hit something cold on the ground and I looked down to see the notebook. Picking it up, I slid it inside my leather bag before heading to the bathroom.

"Did you dream about Jace?" Dick asked, sitting on the edge of the toilet, feet swinging energetically underneath him.

"No."

"I did."

"No, you didn't."

"Maybe I did, how do you know?" he quacked indignantly.

"Because you're still me. Somewhere inside there."

"What if I wasn't? What if it was like a Pinocchio scenario and I wished upon the dead notebook of Jace that I was a real little duck and then you had to take care of me and I was your pet?" He grinned as wide as he could.

"That's not a thing," I called as I left the bathroom and grabbed my things to go downstairs.

I re-read the text from Barbara to make sure I had all the information correct. I was supposed to meet Lee at the weird wild west Starbucks on Sunset at three. I managed to finish my errands and make it back to Hollywood in record time.

Opening the door of the coffee shop, I scanned the tables for Lee. She was sitting in the corner, staring at her iPad. She didn't notice me as I approached until I was right at the table.

"Oh my god, Johnny, hi!"

She stood to wrap me in a hug before we sat. Her long black hair was pulled high in a ponytail on her head that pushed against my chin as we hugged.

"Do you want anything?"

"Yeah, actually, I'll be back."

I stood to go to the register and the kid in front of me had a *Dick* t-shirt on.

"Does that fuck you up?" Dick asked next to me.

Not really.

"It would fuck me up."

You are me.

"But if I wasn't you. It would fuck me up."

Okay.

"Especially because you know Jace hated that. He didn't want the merch."

"He wanted the money," I said out loud before stopping myself.

I was sure to carve out a merchandise clause in our contract with the network because I knew how much stupid merch would feature Dick's stupid face. Merch money would go so much further than residuals ever would.

I studied the shirt. It was one in particular that he hated. Dick, but in psychedelic colors. *It doesn't even have anything to do with Dick,* he argued. He wasn't wrong, but fighting to get approval over any design that was released wasn't possible. So we saw iterations of our child morphed and mass distributed without any control over it.

Jace was the furthest thing I could have imagined from a purist, but that fight lasted nearly a week.

The kid turned slightly once he had ordered and didn't give me a second glance. I never assumed someone would know who I was, since our faces never appeared with anything associated with *Dick* in general, but there was always this slight egotistical pain when someone held a piece of my soul and didn't even know what they carried.

But that was the catch with creating something—it was

mine to give but once someone else received it, I had to let every piece of me that it held, go. I no longer had a say in how it was received or appreciated, no matter how dear to me it was.

"Nice shirt," I quipped.

"Thanks," he replied before moving down the line.

"Can I help you?" the barista asked.

"Black coffee."

"Anything else?"

My eyes ran along the case of food. "A chocolate croissant. Thanks."

"Jesus Christ, you're pathetic," Dick said as he flapped up to stand on the counter.

I pulled out my phone to ignore him.

"You can't ignore me."

Dick began kicking the stacks of cups that were sitting behind the plastic barrier. The noise caused me to look up as tiny animated cups flew around us loudly.

"John?" a barista called out and I watched as the little cups disappeared into thin air.

Grabbing my coffee, I headed back to the table where Lee was waiting. Before sitting, I glanced around to pinpoint Dick. He settled in a seat next to a gorgeous brunette. His little eyes became animated hearts as he stared up at her. Whatever.

"Are you okay?" she asked cautiously.

"I'm okay."

"I heard about Wiley."

"Yeah," I said simply. "It happens I guess."

"Still, it's shit."

"Yeah, thanks." I took a sip of coffee. "So, how are you doing? What are you working on now?"

"We're in post on the feature for Dillon Thomas."

"Oh, nice," I said with as genuine a smile as I could offer.

"That's not what I wanted to talk to you about though. I

had a meeting with Kevin Tyler at Comedy Central and your name came up."

"In what context?" I asked.

She smiled. "All good, I promise. He's a big fan of yours. He wanted to meet with you on a potential show—live action. Would you be interested?"

"I don't know." I rubbed my chin and leaned away from the table.

She closed her iPad and took a drink. Absentmindedly, I tapped my finger against the plastic tabletop.

"Just take the meeting," Lee offered. "What's the harm there?"

"I really want to. And need the work. But it does still feel like a betrayal of some kind."

"Listen," she said, leaning forward as she did, "you've got to learn to live again. You can't let this keep you from doing what you love."

"That's just it. I don't love it anymore." I could see the hurt on her face as I admitted it. "I don't love any of it anymore."

"I'm so sorry to hear that."

"Yeah, I mean, I don't know," I replied quietly as I pushed my coffee cup around the top of the table. "I don't know who I am yet on my own. And I don't like this the way I used to. So maybe it's time for me to do something else. Like get a farm and raise goats or something?"

"Or ducks?" Dick yelled from across the room.

"Or ducks."

"Ducks?" Lee said, unsure before she got the joke. "Ah, yeah, ducks. Funny. You can let this derail you or you can use it. You know Adam's struggle, right?"

I nodded, though it hadn't occurred to me until she brought it up that her husband's previously attempted suicide was probably doing a number to her internally in the wake of Jace's death.

"Yikes," Dick said, quieter than before.

"Afterwards, he went on this great spiritual journey. Mainly with facing his demons with his own dad in Key West—it was a whole thing. And I was grateful he did, because it helped him. But sometimes, I don't think he realized that a lot of us were still stuck behind him. I didn't go on the journey he went on. And most days I was still in that bathroom, looking at his bleeding body. It's not his fault, I know that, but—" her voice broke. "It's *a lot*, Johnny, to carry the weight of others with you. When you can't. In that sense, it's time that you let Jace go."

She was right; I knew she was.

"I don't know how," I admitted quietly, hoping Dick couldn't hear me.

She reached out to touch my hand from across the table. "It's different for everyone. For me, I had to remind myself daily that it was okay to let it go. I got to where I was driving myself crazy."

"So, you're saying I should go to Key West?" I asked and she laughed a sad laugh. "I know what you mean."

"Take the meeting," she urged. "Do something for yourself. That's a good place to start."

"Yeah, for sure. Can you send me Kevin's contact and I'll reach out to schedule it?"

"Of course."

I leaned back in the chair and looked over to where Dick had been sitting, but he was gone.

"Can I ask you something?"

"Of course," she replied as she typed up the email.

"Do you worry about Adam? Now, I mean?"

Her mouth drew into a little line. "Sometimes. That doesn't

go away, you know? I think he is aware, now, of what his bad looks like and how to try and stop it before it gets there. I think socially we don't like to think of depression as a health problem like cancer or arthritis, but that's really what it is. And I personally think of it like an addiction. It's something that a lot of the afflicted have to fight against their whole life. Just because they are in remission at the moment, doesn't mean it's not something that they don't have to constantly battle."

"Right."

"I do worry that we can do everything we possibly can to fight his illness and it won't be enough. I worry about that all the time."

I guess I had never really stepped back enough to look at Jace's life in that context. He had been fighting his illness his whole life. "Thanks. For everything."

She stood when I did and gave me a hug. "Call me if you need anything."

As I made my way back out into the sunlight, I noticed the kid in the *Dick* shirt leaving in front of me. I slid my sunglasses on and watched him joking with his friend as he got into a car, taking a piece of my life with him.

"Ready?" Dick said next to me, following my gaze.

"Sure," I replied, heading toward my Prius.

———

For some reason I was incredibly conscious of how *empty* the conference room was. We normally had staff meetings there full of easygoing laughter and bits that would run for hours until someone stopped them. But now, it was silent, quiet, dead.

I looked in my bag for paper and pen and the idea almost made me laugh. Like I was going to take notes. I was going to talk to the man taking over my show and take notes on what he said as though it mattered.

My fingers slid over Jace's notebook and I pulled it out from my bag and set it on the table in front of me.

Jace walked in, rubbing his hand through his hair as he did. "What are you doing in here so late?"

I leaned back in the chair, bobbing up and down. "I'm stuck on episode three. It sucks."

He crossed his arms over the back of the chair directly across from me at the table. "So, don't do it."

"Don't write the episode?"

"Yeah," he nodded, pushing his glasses up against the bridge of his nose. "What would happen if you didn't?"

"I'd get fired."

"You can't get fired," he shot back. "Who is going to fire you?"

"The network?"

"Oh," he replied as he sat down. "Yeah, you're probably right. What have you got?"

"It's the one where he goes undercover as a mailman."

"Why?"

"It's funny?"

"Is it?"

I tilted my head in exasperation and Jace laughed his loudest laugh. "You look like a puppy when you do that."

"You're not helping."

"Not yet, give it time. I'm a slow release capsule on occasion. Are you wanting a different premise or to punch up the bit?"

"I don't even know anymore," I admitted.

"What's the main joke of the mailman bit?"

"Bramblebutt chasing him—because he's a dog?"

"Low fruit," Jace said quickly. "What else?"

"Anthrax."

"Jesus Christ."

"Bramblebutt gets the Anthrax that Dick is investigating. So then they are in isolation in the hospital together. It's sweet in the end."

"Gross," Jace replied, leaning back and looking up at the ceiling of the conference room. "Do you ever think about dying? What happens to *Dick* when we die?"

"Are we dying at the same time in this scenario?"

"For sure."

"Then who cares?"

He laughed. "Okay, so let's say only one of us dies."

"I have no idea. I guess it depends on what happens and who is dying. The likelihood of us dying before *Dick* is pretty low. He might die pretty quickly if I don't finish this episode."

His mouth curled up at the edges. "Okay, let's say *Dick* dies."

"In the show or real life?"

"Real life."

"Then what?"

"That's what I'm asking."

He began turning slowly in his chair, still looking up at the ceiling.

"Then we do something else? Make something else?" I offered.

"Promise?"

"Promise."

"Alright." He stopped spinning and slapped the conference room table loudly. "Bramblebutt should get the Anthrax, but Dick shouldn't. Dick should think he's dying. And then in the end after his big confession of how he actually cares for him, we find out it wasn't Anthrax, it was flour, or coke, whichever is funnier. And once he realizes he's fine, he recants his feelings. But Bramblebutt won't let it go and lords it over him."

When he was finished, he stood with both hands out.

"That will work."

It did, but it didn't. Hearing Jace say it made me realize that it should be a one-sided confession that only the audience knows. In the final cut of the Anthrax episode, Dick did get the fake Anthrax—we landed on coke—and thinks he's dying. So he writes out a long confession, but it never makes it to Bramblebutt. Once he finds out he's fine, he tears it up. Bramblebutt never knew how Dick really felt, leaving a tiny taste of sorrow for the viewers to relish when the episode was over.

When he read it, Jace told me I nailed it. He was never possessive over ideas like that. All of our ideas were shared, no matter what form it ended up in. And my best ideas weren't really mine—or good—until Jace had a pass on it.

I would miss that.

I would miss it so much.

The door opened and Wiley walked in, pulling me suddenly back to the empty conference room and the reality in which Jace was dead and I was alone and Wiley was taking over the show that we had carefully put every little piece of our being into.

"Hey Johnny," he said with a little too much joy, extending his hand.

I stood and shook it, still internally rattled by my daydreaming.

"Hey there."

"Is this good or do you want to go somewhere else?"

I debated asking if we could move to Jace's office in the bitchiest power move I could possibly think, but decided against it.

"Do it," Dick said as he laid on top of the table, looking up at the lights overhead. "I dare you."

"This is fine," I said instead.

"I'm glad we're getting a chance to meet. I've been a real fan of yours for years."

"Yeah, thanks."

"We had to write a paper over *Midnight Dolly* in one of my film writing classes. I was so enthralled by it. Is that weird to say?"

It was, but I wouldn't have said that. "Oh. Okay."

"It's also kind of weird to be in this position. Coming in the way I am and under the circumstances and all."

"Yeah."

"I did want to let you know I'm going to do everything in my power to preserve the memory of Jace in this creation. It's still from the minds of you and him. It's one hundred percent still a Johnny and Jace piece of art. That will never change."

I wanted to sigh. It already had changed.

The reality was the show was no longer what it was supposed to be the minute Jace took his last breath. It wasn't Wiley's fault. He was just doing his job.

"I appreciate that," I heard myself reply.

"And I have the bible, and scripts, and about as much information as I think I could possibly have on this. All I'm missing is your brain. If I could borrow that for a while and get whatever is there, that would be great."

He laughed an obnoxious laugh and I forced as much of a smile as I could.

"Well, I'm still using it for now."

He laughed louder at this, pointing at me. "That's a good one. Good one, sir."

I nearly threw up when he used the word *sir*. This needed to end. Immediately. I saw Dick sneaking up behind him with his favorite weapon of choice—a rope noose—creeping quietly from the corner of the office. His eyes were drawn together in a little V and his pupils were red.

"Okay," I said, standing and quickly picking up Jace's notebook. "I've got another appointment I've got to run to. But I'm glad we got a chance to meet. I have full confidence in your ability to move forward and I'm excited to have the opportunity to work with you as we continue."

I stuck out my hand and watched Dick's beak fall off behind him in shock.

Wiley grinned as he shook my hand vigorously. "Want me to walk you out?"

"No, I know my way around the building," I joked and he laughed harder than he should have again.

"I'll see you around, Wiley."

As soon as we were in the elevator, Dick flapped up to perch on the little metal bar that ran around the perimeter of the space. "What the fuck was that?"

I turned to him with a furrowed brow. "You're *surprised?* How did you manage that one? Or are you a better actor than we thought you were?"

"Fuck off. He's a moron."

"I know."

"And he's going to destroy our show."

"I know."

"So what are you going to do about it?"

"Nothing," I said with a smile as the elevator doors opened and I walked outside into the sun, relishing the feeling of the warmth on my cheeks. "Absolutely nothing."

11

The Unreliable Narrator

I sat in the waiting area, nervous. It had been a while since I had gone to a pitch meeting, especially on my own. While working on *Dick*, Jace and I had pursued other things, but always together. And during the last season especially, we had been pretty singularly focused on that. I think part of me really felt like we had two or three more seasons in us at a minimum, and it would be years before we'd be pitching again.

Jace was often the hype man of the meeting, wowing the execs with jokes and confidence. I thought back to our original pitch of *Dick*.

"Why are you so nervous?" Jace asked, looking down at my shaking leg.

"We just really need this."

"You're not going to tell them that," he said quickly. "Listen, they need us. They need this show or their network will fall apart. That's the reality for them. They don't even know how much they need it. They need it bad, Johnny, they need it real bad."

He had switched to his horrifyingly bad Elvis voice that he always used when he knew I needed to calm down. He loved doing it because he could emphasize the Johnny as 'Jahn-neh' and it never failed to make me laugh.

It wasn't true, but that was the reality of Jace. He made things true simply by saying them, something I could never do. And when he said it and believed it, usually I did too.

They called us back and Jace flashed me a wicked smile before we entered into the conference room. I had brought our portfolio with various iterations of Dick in shiny Technicolor prints. They were Jace's drawings, but I was the one in charge of making sure they were printed, organized and ready for the world to see.

"How's it going, Phil? Can I call you Phil?"

Phillip Gorman laughed before reaching out to shake Jace's hand. "I saw your short film. Very funny."

"That's all this guy right here," Jace said, pointing to me.

"Oh yeah? Great work."

"Thanks."

"That's what you get with Jace and Johnny. You're getting two writers for the price of one."

"Alright, jumping right in?" Phil asked as he sat down.

"That's all I know, man. In this business, we get thirty seconds to show you what we can do. Thirty seconds to make a first and last impression. In thirty seconds you can see two men sitting in front of you, trying so desperately to get our little show made, and for us this means everything. For us, these thirty seconds will last an eternity—everything we've been working for in the last ten years rests all in these thirty seconds and whether or not you'll give us the chance that we feel we're finally ready for. But for you? It's another meeting in your day before you finally get to go home and take your shoes off."

Jace's phone alarm went off.

"Stop it," Phil said, laughing loudly and slapping his desk. "You set a damn timer?"

Jace grinned as he pulled out his phone and pointed it at Phil to show that his thirty seconds were up.

"I hope you write as good as he pitches," Phil said in an aside to me.

"Even better," Jace said, raising his hand to slap my knee. "Johnny can weave a story nicer than your grandmother's crocheted table runner."

Phil laughed again.

"Who all is involved?"

It was the question that usually brought the wall upon us. The truth was, we didn't have big name voices and we didn't have a shiny production company willing to put money behind us.

"Phil Gorman. We got Phil Gorman involved."

It was the first time I'd heard him use that line and even I couldn't stop a little laugh as Phil slapped his desk again.

"Very good. That's very good. You're so green though, we'd want a pretty big stake, businesswise. You've never run a show before. Hell, have you ever run a writer's room before?"

"We're quick learners and Johnny here is the most organized son-of-a-bitch I've ever met. Did I mention you're getting both of our brains for the price of one?"

"Listen, this was a courtesy call. I already wanted your show before you walked in this door. I think it's hilarious. Send me your pilot and we'll see what we can do to get this shit show optioned."

I tried not to react as I felt Jace's foot slide over to tap against mine.

"We can do that. We'll have our agent send over the script next week. We'll do everything we possibly can to live up to the trust that you've given us here today."

"Alright," Phil said, standing and extending his very large hand. "You've already sold me, you don't have to keep trying. Get me the script and we'll make some money."

"You got it," Jace said, grabbing the hand as firmly as he could.

We walked out into the hall and I heard Jace say very quietly, "Don't do anything in case he's watching."

Silently, we walked to the elevator and Jace pressed the button with more calm than I had ever seen him possess in his entire life.

"All good," I said softly, shoving my hands in my pockets. "Totally chill."

"Yeah, you know," he said, biting his lower lip. "We're calm and collected."

The elevator dinged loudly and we slowly sauntered into the elevator with no cares in the world. As soon as the door closed, Jace exploded in a flurry of movement and grabbed my arms frantically.

"We fucking did it!" he yelled, jumping up and down. "We mother-fucking did it!"

"*You* did it," I emphasized.

"JAHNNEH," he screamed, full Elvis mode activated. "I can't fucking believe it Jahnneh. We're gonna be famous Jahnneh—our names in lights. Right on the Vegas strip, Jahnneh."

I couldn't tell if I was laughing, crying or both. None of it felt real in that moment. Jace was laughing and still gripped my elbows like he was holding on for dear life.

When the doors opened, a man in a stiff, black, business suit was standing there, watching us carefully, unsure of what was happening. Jace's laughter renewed and he drug me by my elbows out of the elevator.

"This is it," he said. "Remember this very fucking day, Jonathan Goodwin. This is the fucking day we finally made it. This is the beginning of everything." He stared at me with a gleam in his ocean blue eyes and that was the first time I understood how deep I'd allowed him to crawl into the inner chambers of my heart. While he held onto my elbows, he had no idea he was really holding on to my entire being and that us being connected in this way was truly the only thing that mattered to me anymore. It was irrational and unexplainable, but it was there."

I wasn't even sure what to say. No words could explain the excitement, fear, joy and terror that was starting to lodge in my stomach. An option wasn't a deal, but this was the furthest in the door we'd ever gotten anywhere with a network. And a network meant stability and *money.*

"Oh my god," I said finally.

"Come on, let's get a drink. I've got to call Riley."

"Let's go."

He paused to look at me. "Johnny?"

I looked at the door to the waiting area where I was sitting. I was sitting, waiting for Kevin. To talk about a new project. Jace wasn't here, that was a memory. Jace had been dead now for almost two months, but it seemed like yesterday we were pitching *Dick.* Yesterday...

"Johnny?" the girl repeated.

"Johnny?" Dick yelled at my feet.

I blinked several times before standing, ignoring Dick as he waddled behind us. I followed the smartly dressed woman into the open space office. A few of the people looked up to watch me as I passed, but there was none of the critical judgment I had feared before entering.

"Johnny Goodwin," Kevin said, standing as I entered and extending his hand.

"Thank you for being willing to meet with me," I offered as I sat down. "I'm sure it's not the original plan."

"It is, actually," Kevin said as he picked up his pen. "We really wanted to work with you."

"Right, but I'm no Jace."

Kevin cleared his throat before continuing, "Jonathan, I don't know how to say this, man, without hurting you, but Jace was a total dick. He had no respect for this industry and your work. His reputation was starting to catch up with him and..." he trailed off.

"Asshole," Dick mumbled.

"Yeah, well," I started, "I know. I mean, I always knew who Jace was."

"You get it."

"You get it? Of course you get it." Dick laughed. "Fucking prick."

"Yeah..." I nodded. "I do get it."

"I heard about Christian. I wouldn't take that personally."

I leaned back in the seat, finally allowing myself to relax a little. "It's hard not to."

Kevin smiled. "Right. My first show I was running by myself was a nightmare. I hated every minute of it. It's a beast of a job."

I nodded, not really sure how to respond.

"What are you working on these days?" Kevin asked.

"*Dick*, mostly. Season 3 is in pre-production."

"No, I mean, what are you working on? Like something just for you. It doesn't even have to be work. Just for fun."

I heard the sentence float to the bottom of my brain. Just for fun. I hadn't written just for fun in years.

"Nothing, really."

I saw the strain on Kevin's face and felt like I was disappointing him somehow.

"What would you write if you had no limits—no budget, no deadlines, no outside influences?"

"I did have this idea," I started, leaning forward. Dick shifted to get closer. "It's a like a rom-com, I guess, where Jesus and Judas are lovers."

Kevin laughed.

"But not like Bible, Jesus, you know," I started, "Like he's a con man—a magician. And Judas knows and doesn't care, because he loves him. And in the end it all goes horribly wrong, as we know. I don't know. It's been in my brain a long time."

Jace always hated it—Dick reminded me.

"That's funny," Kevin said leaning back in his chair. "That's really funny. Who is your Jesus?"

"I don't know." I raised a shoulder casually.

"Just spitball. Who would you get?"

"Like a Pedro Pascal type would be my dream."

Kevin clapped loudly. "Love it. And your Judas?"

I thought for a moment, or at least wanted to appear to Kevin that I was. The truth was, I had written almost all of it in my head over the last two years. I guess I thought if nothing touched the paper, it was fine, since we weren't actually working on it. And Jace had already rejected it.

"Colin Hanks."

"Colin Hanks and Pedro Pascal as biblical lovers. God damn, Johnny, I want that show. Write me that show."

I laughed and brushed my hands over my pants leg. "Yeah, that's funny."

"I'm being serious. Get me a pilot. You've got three weeks."

My laughter stopped. "Are you serious?"

"I just said I was. I like you, Johnny. You're funny, reliable, and a really good writer. It's time you make the thing you've always wanted to make. For you."

I tapped my palm on my knee, unsure how to respond. I knew what he meant, but the reality was that now I would only make things I wanted to make because there was no second person alive to consider. People were treating it like some kind of break up, but it really wasn't. I knew if Jace was alive, I would have been sitting at a desk with him, scribbling note after note on what did and didn't work about Clem. We didn't break up—we were separated.

"Absolutely," I said, standing. "I'll have it to you in three weeks."

We shook hands and as I left I looked around to see if the little fowl was following, but noticed he was gone.

I didn't have anyone to celebrate with. It was only me, alone in the hallway.

"Can I help you?" the woman who had shown me back into the office asked from her desk.

"I think I just sold a pilot?" I offered.

"Congratulations."

It was sincere, but also kind of sad.

I considered calling Riley, but thought against it. I pulled my phone out to text Yuto, but stopped myself before I even started. It wasn't like he had any reason to care, and telling him so I would have someone tell me how great I was felt stupid.

I started to go down the mental rabbit hole of what Jace would say or think—if he would play the role of supportive friend or knock it down as a jealous saboteur. Before I got too deep in my own fantastical delusions, I brushed all of those thoughts away. It didn't matter what I thought Jace would have thought. Jace would never know because he was dead.

None of that mattered. I had a show to write.

"Emmys," Dick said.

"What?"

"FLASH FORWARD!" Dick cried as he snapped his little feathers together.

We stood in the hallway, staring at one another.

"What the hell was that?"

Dick looked around. "I said flash forward. That's supposed to move us to the next plot point."

"That's lazy. It's a lazy writing trick when the writer can't figure out how to transition from one scene to another."

Yuto adjusted his bowtie as he got inside the car. "You look nice."

"Fuck."

"What?"

"Nothing," I said, rubbing my forehead. "I should have taken some ibuprofen or something. I'm already getting a headache."

"Hold on," he said quickly before jumping out of the car to go back inside his house.

He was gone only a matter of minutes, but returned with a little plastic bottle in his hand.

"Thank you," I said with a smile.

"Of course. It's the big night. No headaches or bad times allowed. We're going to the freaking Emmys!"

I laughed. "It's just the Creative Arts Emmys."

"'Just the Creative Arts Emmys'? None of that, Jonathan. It's still a super cool awards show."

"Yeah, okay, but don't expect to see all the A-listers here. Most of them won't show. It's three o'clock in the afternoon."

He leaned back in his seat and laughed as he pulled out his phone to take a picture of us.

"What are you doing?"

"Come on, I've got to document this whole experience for you."

"You look really nice," I offered, letting my eyes take in his perfectly tailored suit.

"Thanks. You clean up pretty well yourself. Hey, do we need any ground rules?"

"Ground rules?"

"Yeah, like, am I your date? Officially?"

I laughed. "Yes, if you're okay with that."

"One hundred percent. So it's okay if we *act* like we're on a date?"

Hoping my face wasn't as red as it felt, I scratched my neck nervously and nodded, feeling like a teenager going to prom. "Yeah, I'm okay with that. If you are."

"Oh yeah, I am. If I overstep or anything, let me know. I don't want to make you uncomfortable."

I was beginning to think it wasn't possible for Yuto to make me uncomfortable. I was awkward, in general, but with him, it was starting to feel safe. At least, safer than I allowed myself to feel with any boyfriend before.

A contented silence settled between us before my phone buzzed in my pocket. Pulling it out, I saw Riley's name.

"What's up?"

"Are you here yet?"

"Almost," I answered, looking at the traffic crowding the street.

"I'm assuming we're sitting together?"

"Yeah, I would think so."

"Okay. I'm going to wait outside for you. I don't want to walk in alone," she said distractedly.

"You didn't bring anyone?" I asked.

"Yeah, Penny's here."

"Got it. Okay. We're close."

"We?"

I could hear the hesitation in her voice.

"I'm bringing a date," I said, and didn't know why I felt weird about it.

"Oh. Okay. See you soon."

I heard the click of the call and let my phone rest in my lap.

"Everything okay?" Yuto asked.

"Yeah, so, we'll be with Jace's wife." I paused, trying to figure out if I was supposed to word it differently. Jace's widow?

"Riley?"

I nodded.

It was weird because there was no normal timeline where Jace and I weren't getting ready and going together. We should have been together. Riley and I showing up separately would have never happened otherwise. Last time we all had coordinating outfits.

"What's it like? With you and Riley?" he asked.

I looked down, unsure what to say. "I don't know. I mean. At the moment, strained? I guess?"

"Why?"

I pursed my lips, unable to answer. Should I blurt out that I was in love with Jace and Riley knew that for sure now? And maybe I held a special piece of Jace's life too? Should I explain that we were connected somehow in ways that I probably blew out of proportion when Jace was alive and grasped onto for dear life now that he was gone? That I made him my reason for getting up every morning and the last thought on my mind when I went to bed at night?

"I think we're just both a little lost right now."

He nodded. "I think after Eva died, it was weird being around friends that we only knew as a couple. Like I wasn't sure the reason why we hung out still existed. In some ways, it felt like a divorce."

"Yeah," I lied. "That's probably it."

The car slowed as it pulled up to the Peacock Theater. Yuto

began straining to see those standing around the cameras and lights.

"Ready?" I asked.

"Is there a red carpet?" he asked, amazed.

I smiled. "Yes. There is."

"Let's do this."

When we got out of the car, he began walking around, aimlessly filming things on his phone. I called Riley.

"Where are you?" I asked, scanning the crowd.

"I'm by the first step and repeat. My hand is in the air."

My eyes darted back and forth as I looked for a wildly waving Black arm. It worked and I pulled on Yuto's sleeve as we headed toward her.

"Hey," she said as we got near, adjusting the strap of her red gown.

"Johnny," Penny said with more coldness than I expected.

It seemed that Riley had filled her sister in on everything.

"Ready?" Riley asked.

I debated dragging her to the side and hashing it all out right there. I hated this awkward space that I wasn't really sure was as deserved as she thought it was.

Was it really so bad? I wanted to ask.

We got in line for the red carpet. One thing that was never shown on TV was the lines. You had to stand in line to walk the carpet and stand in line to get in and stand in line to get your seat. It was one thing that Jace hated, being as antsy as he always was. Yuto, on the other hand, was spinning slowly, filming everything around him.

"Johnny," he started, moving closer, "is that Joel McHale?"

I looked at the tall figure hunched over by another man's face, listening to whatever was being said. It was hard to tell, but I guessed it probably was.

"I think so," I said before pulling my phone out of my pocket.

"So, how did you two meet?" Riley asked as we shifted forward.

"We met at a grief group. My wife died six years ago and I go to this support group."

"Oh," Riley said, surprised, turning with her hand pointing to me. "The one...?"

I nodded. "I went without you."

"Oh," she said again.

Yuto looked from her to me but didn't say anything.

"It was nice."

"So, you lost your wife?" Riley asked. She raised her eyebrow at this and I knew it was more toward me than Yuto. *You have a type.* I could hear her quip.

"Yeah, septic shock. It was awful. I'm so sorry for your loss. I've heard a little about Jace from Johnny."

"I bet you have," Riley said with a smile that didn't reach her eyes.

It was finally our turn and we walked down the red carpet, pausing on the little marks and letting the photographers do their thing. I enjoyed the spectacle of anything Hollywood, but mainly because of how Jace always reacted to it. He pretended to hate the demand of all the steps and procedures, but the minute he was on a red carpet he was acting like a fool and energizing anyone around him.

"I can't believe this," Yuto said next to me.

I reached out and took his hand as we moved to the next mark and I heard a flurry of camera clicks when I did. The gays being gay always seemed to be a source of paparazzi fodder.

He gave my hand a quick squeeze as he stopped at the final point. I handed over our tickets and waited for Riley. A few people stopped us and offered their condolences for Jace.

"Are you doing okay?" Yuto asked.

"Yeah," I lied, pulling down on my suit jacket as we walked.

"I'm going to run to the restroom before we go sit down."

"Sure," I said, pointing in the direction of the bathrooms.

As soon as he was gone, Riley moved closer. "Are you dating?"

"Kind of. We've met up a few times and I made it clear I was asking him on a date here."

She nodded and looked like she wanted to say something else, but didn't. "We're going to go sit down."

I stuck my hands in my pockets and moved toward the wall to wait for Yuto. When he returned, we started back into the theater. Loud music was playing when we walked in and he was practically bouncing up and down with excitement. It was incredibly endearing.

I found our table where Riley was already sitting with Mark and Toni. Another couple sat next to them, but they looked only vaguely familiar to me.

"Do you remember last time we were here?" Riley asked, raising one eyebrow with a slight smile as I sat down.

"I do."

Yuto looked between us. "What happened?"

"There was an incident."

"Oh," Riley said after taking a drink of her champagne, "not just an incident. Jace slapped Johnny's date in the face."

"I'm sorry, what?" Yuto asked, leaning forward. "Slapped?"

"Yeah," Riley said with a sarcastic grin. "He slapped him right across the face."

"Why?"

"They got into a fight," I said simply.

"Tell him the whole story," Riley replied.

I looked to Riley, unsure what she was wanting. Penny leaned around her, also interested.

"They got into some kind of drinking contest or something. Jace and Blake, actually, you know Blake—from the coffee shop?"

"Oh, yeah," Yuto agreed.

I ignored Riley's frantic look of confusion at the words 'from the coffee shop.' "Well Blake accused Jace of cheating. It became a whole thing. We had to separate them by the end of the night."

"That's not exactly why Jace slapped him," Riley offered.

"What really happened?" Penny jumped in.

"I don't know what you mean," I said, ready to talk about literally anything else.

"Blake called you a bitch. After you refused to take his side against Jace. You really don't remember that?"

"I do remember that."

Penny raised an eyebrow. "Seriously?"

"That is what happened," I confessed.

"You really can't see it, can you?" Riley asked.

"See what?"

"He was defending *your honor*. He was standing up *for you*."

I leaned back in my chair. "Okay."

Yuto's face was flashing back and forth, watching each of us carefully, as though afraid to get in the middle of it.

"How did you guys meet Jace?" he asked in both mine and Riley's direction.

"College," I said quickly.

"An event in Beverly Hills."

"Now, now," I started. "Why don't you tell *that* full story?"

Riley's eyes grew wide. "You can fuck right off."

"Riley," Penny gasped.

"Oh, so Penny hasn't heard that one?"

I looked Riley square in the eyes as she slowly shook her

head. One thing about knowing someone as long as we had was the guarantee of mutual destruction if we really wanted it.

"Riley was bartending. And Jace was her patron."

"What's so bad about that?" Penny asked.

Riley looked at me, pleading.

"Because she ended up leaving with him. Quit her shift right then and there. I guess it was love at first sight," I offered, taking a sip from the water glass in front of me.

"That's not that bad," Penny returned, sitting back in her seat, disappointed from not getting the tea she had hoped on her sister.

The full story was that Riley was working the event as a bottle service girl. And once she served Jace he took her to the back room and they hooked up before they left, leaving Jace's date at the table. It was apparently love at first sight for both of them.

A man walked up and offered his hand. I knew that I knew who he was, but his identity was escaping me. I smiled and shook his extended hand politely.

"Congrats on the pilot."

"Oh," I said, surprised. "Thanks?"

The man squinted, as though suddenly worried they said the wrong thing. "You're pitching a pilot to Kevin with Comedy Central, aren't you? That's what the rumor mill told me."

"Yeah," I conceded. "Yeah, actually I am."

Riley looked over at the news, but said nothing.

"Well, congrats, man, that's great."

"Thank you. Hopefully it turns into something."

When they left, Riley turned to Penny. "I'm going to get a drink. Want something?"

"I'll go with you," Penny replied quickly, lifting her skirt to push her chair back.

As soon as they were gone, I felt Yuto slapping my leg. "What the heck, Johnny. You didn't tell me you sold a pilot?"

"It's not a big deal," I said, pushing my glass in front of me.

"It's a huge deal. What are you talking about?" He moved his hand up this time to my shoulder, shaking me gently. "Why didn't you tell me?"

"I don't know."

Yuto leaned forward so far I thought he was going to try to kiss me. "You're allowed to be proud of yourself."

"I know."

My eyes trailed down to his lips and I wondered what he would do if I tried to kiss him. He noticed where my eyes went and grinned before leaning back in his chair. "We'll celebrate later. Next time you get really amazing good news, will you tell me please?"

"Sure," I said with a smile.

"Did he say you sold a pilot?" Mark called from across the table interrupting our intimate moment.

"Yeah, maybe. Well, not really. I just pitched something to Comedy Central."

"Huh."

I wanted to tell Mark that maybe if he didn't want me pitching to Comedy Central that he shouldn't have hired a showrunner to kick me off my own show. I wanted to tell him that I wasn't going to be around much longer and us being together in that moment was likely one of the last times it would ever happen. But instead I smiled, and said nothing.

The show started and I felt like I was going to throw up. It finally registered why we were all sitting around a table together and there was an actual possibility that *Dick* was going to win an award. The first time we had gotten nominated for anything, I allowed myself to enjoy being invited to the room where it all took place. I never had as much faith in our work as

Jace did and he was convinced on our first nomination that we were going to win. He prepared a speech and everything.

When we lost, it devastated him. Ups and downs. It was always extreme ups and downs with him. That was a down, down.

So, for this night, I had prepared nothing. I was allowing myself to be present in the room with no expectations. I was going to enjoy the good things and the bad as they came. The longer the show droned on, the more I was able to tune out. Eventually, we arrived at the "In Memoriam" section where they showed pictures and honored all the dead celebrities who had passed over the year. Barbara had warned us that Jace was going to be included.

I knew it was coming, but I don't think any of us were actually prepared for it. When the black and white picture of Jace's face popped up, I burst into laughter. *In memoriam*—it read, with *Jace Van Noy—writer* in beautiful script underneath it. The picture they used had to have been one they found on the Internet. It was a headshot, but not one of the actual professional ones he had made. It was one that he had done at JCPenny's as a joke—it was a glam shot. Jace's final bit.

"Oh my god," Riley gasped next to me.

I gripped my sides, trying desperately to control the laughter in case a stray camera panned our way while his giant, airbrushed face loomed over us. He was genuinely glowing.

"Did you do this?" Penny hissed quietly.

I shook my head and the picture flipped to an older actress who had passed. Hers was a very traditional headshot.

"That's Jace though," I said loud enough for them to hear.

He would have found it so funny. I remember that day at the studio when he was posing like a teenager going to prom. He wanted to use those headshots all the time and Barbara had to fight him over it regularly.

"He would have loved that," Riley said, shifting in her chair and finishing her glass.

We watched the rest of the tribute in silence, listening to the swell of the music around us. It was such an odd thing to sit around, watching the images of the dead together. I didn't even know some of them had passed. And others I didn't even know who they were. I wondered how many thought that about Jace as he appeared.

"You okay?" Yuto asked next to me.

"Yeah. I'm good."

It was a fitting tribute to the life Jace lived.

Our category was one of the last and when it finally arrived, I had already stopped listening halfway through the speech about the creative expansion of animation in the arts.

"And the nominees are..."

This phrase caught my attention. When they said the word *Dick*, I looked up, feeling Riley's hand slip into mine. My heart began to race as the words tumbled from the stage.

"And the Emmy for short form animated program goes to: *Dick*—'Manthrax Unlimited'."

The words echoed in my head as I registered what was happening. There was applause around the room and I looked to Riley.

"Go on," she said, clapping along with the rest of them.

Normally it would have been me and Jace. It would have been the whole team. Jace would have bounced up the stairs, laughing the whole way and wowing the crowd with jokes and bullshit about how stupid it all was while basking in the glow of creative victory.

I pushed my chair back and started to walk, trying to focus on making sure my feet didn't trip over one another as I walked. *How much time do they give? What do I say? Am I going to throw up?*

I took the statue from Jennifer Coolidge and moved to the microphone. Suddenly, I was incredibly conscious of everyone staring at me from the seats down below.

"Um, wow," I said looking down at the statue in my hand. It was heavier than I thought it would be. "We have an amazing team and so many people to thank but I'm sorry I'm not going to do that. I know I wouldn't be up here if it wasn't for a big missing piece of tonight and that's Jason Van Noy. We lost Jace earlier this year and this is all his. I hope he's somewhere here, watching and laughing. We love you and miss you so much, buddy. Check on your family and friends, tell them how much you love them. It can never be enough. Thank you."

There was more applause as I made my way back down the steps to our table. It all had to occur within the span of two minutes, but it felt like hours that I was creeping forward and scrutinized bit by bit by those around me.

Finally back at my seat, I put the statue on the table and felt Yuto's hand on my knee give a squeeze. Mark and Toni gushed, each talking barely above a whisper about the moment that just happened, even though we were all witness to it. It felt like slow motion.

My eyes fell to the golden goddess reaching high above her head. This was the arrival. This was the thing that we had worked toward for years and years. And it was so fucking hollow.

Did it even mean anything if Jace wasn't here to see it?

It wasn't supposed to be this way.

The rest of the ceremony passed twice as fast once we were done and over with. When it finished, everyone began moving around the room, taking pictures of their pretty little statues to post on social media for bragging rights.

"I'll be back," I said, gently touching Riley's shoulder as I moved across the room in the direction of Lee Young.

I saw Lee speaking to a tall man in a black cowboy hat that matched his decorated suit. I knew he was an actor, but not one that I could place off the top of my head.

She noticed me approaching and touched the cowboy's arm before acknowledging me.

"Johnny! Hi! Oh my god, congratulations."

"Thanks," I said with a smile.

We hugged and she turned to the cowboy. "You know Paul Osborne."

"Mr. Osborne," I replied, extending a hand.

He shook it with the firm grip you'd expect from someone wearing a cowboy hat at a Hollywood awards show.

"We just wrapped on Dillon Thomas's project."

"Oh yeah?" I asked. "I'm sure that was a fun project. Dillon's fantastic."

The truth was, I hadn't worked with Dillon and only knew he was kind of an asshole, but fantastic was the kind of thing you say to people who can put you in a room.

"Life changing," he said stoically. "Dillon almost died."

I stared, unsure if that was a bit. I guessed Paul didn't do bits.

"Oh. I'm sorry," I looked to Lee for help.

"He's fine. He's here somewhere."

"Okay."

"I'm going to go find him. I'll leave you to it," Paul said, patting Lee on the shoulder before wandering away.

"That was something."

Lee laughed and shook her hands quickly. "Dillon didn't almost die, for the record."

"Right. How are you doing?" I asked, anxious to change the subject.

"I'm hanging in there. What about you? I'm glad to see you here tonight."

"Yeah, thanks. I wanted to say thanks, about Kevin. I'm writing a pilot and it's really helpful, I think, to get space from *Dick* and Jace and all of that. This is something for me and that's honestly kind of freeing."

"That's great. I'm so glad to hear that. Maybe I'll get to work on it? If you want any passes or something, I'd be happy to read."

"Yeah, thanks. Honestly. For helping me out."

She puckered her lips and moved closer before speaking. "I meant what I said before. You're the exception to the rule and the kind of person that everyone loves to work with. I hope you're willing to accept that."

I stuck my hands in my pockets. "Well, hopefully we get to work together on it. And if you need anything from me, let me know."

"Here, let's get a picture," she offered and we swiveled around to get a selfie together with the stage behind us.

She showed me the image when she was done and the smile on my face looked better than it felt.

"See ya soon," I hedged before moving away.

A few other people stopped to offer congratulations and positive thoughts as I made my way back to the table. Yuto and Riley were leaning over my empty seat to talk as I approached. I wondered what it would have been like if Jace had been here. I liked to think he would like Yuto. He certainly wouldn't have slapped him.

"Let's get a picture!" Mark yelled as I approached.

"Let me take it," Yuto offered.

We stood around the table as a group. Mark held the Emmy firmly with both hands. From the outside, you'd never know that the entire group was as fractured as it could be with divisions getting stronger by the minute—a Jenga tower teetering on collapse. The little Jace block had been removed from our lives and we verged on the edge in his absence.

When we were done, Mark handed the Emmy to Riley.

"You should take this."

She looked at it skeptically but then her eyes met mine and she reached over to claim her victory. "Thanks. I'll keep it."

I knew she was trying to hurt me, but I wanted to tell her it wasn't even possible anymore. That nothing she could say or do would hurt me more than the pain I felt from the absence of Jace in my life.

"Alright," Riley said, adjusting the statue in her hands. "I'm not sure if we're doing the afterparty thing. I'm exhausted."

"Understandable."

I glanced to both Penny and Yuto, laughing about something off to the side.

"Are we okay?" I asked finally, shoving my hands in my pockets.

She barely raised a shoulder and looked me dead in my eyes. There was a familiar glaze of detachment that I had seen in my own eyes for the past few weeks.

"I want to be. I really want to be. Outside of Jace, you were really the person closest to me. And I can't afford to lose you both at the same time."

I nodded. "I'm so sorry, Riley. You have to know how sorry I am about everything. I hate having space between us."

"I want it to be like it was before. With me and you and Jace being stupid and having fun. Now I'm *blaming you*. Why am I blaming you?"

"I blame me too," I teased, though it fell flat.

"I don't want to say things I can't take back. And I don't want to be mad at you any more. But I think I need some more time to process it all. You understand."

"Of course." I paused. "Nothing has to change between us though, right?"

She looked at me as though I had slapped her. "Are you serious, Johnny? Everything's changed. Literally everything in my life has changed. And I'm frantically trying to get some of it back and I think, tonight, I'm finally realizing that is never going to happen. It's all broken in a way that can't be repaired. And I fucking hate that."

She was right. I knew she was right.

"Congratulations," she said, moving closer. "I'm sorry tonight was what it was and not what it should have been."

I shrugged. "It's fine."

She raised one hand to adjust her dress strap absent-mindedly.

"You look great, by the way," I said quietly.

"Thanks," she replied.

"Jace would have loved it."

"I was going to file for divorce."

I felt my breath catch in my throat as I processed what she had said. "What?"

"He was right. I was planning on leaving him. I met an attorney and everything. The notebook. He knew. He must have known."

I was conscious of the fact that I was standing there, staring, but didn't know how to accept the information I had been given.

"How right was he?" she asked, her eyes narrowing.

"He was... right about everything," I admitted to myself for the first time. "All of it was true."

"So you were you in love with him?"

I didn't respond. I couldn't.

She nodded slowly, her lips forming a thin line. "Good-bye, John."

I watched her signal to Penny as she walked away. Penny and Yuto gave each other a quick hug before Penny rushed after the retreating Riley. I had a sinking feeling that it would be the last time I ever saw Riley.

"Ready?" I asked Yuto.

He nodded and we followed the crowd in the direction of the door. "Why didn't you get to keep it?"

"I'll get one," I replied. "We'll all get engraved ones with the show and everything on it later."

"Oh. That's like a prop one?"

I grinned as we walked and slipped my hand into his. "Something like that."

"Thank you for inviting me. I can't believe I got to see all of this in person."

"Do you want some ice cream?" I asked. "I'd really love some ice cream."

Yuto smiled and nodded. "Yeah, let's go get some celebratory ice cream."

We were stopped a few more times as we tried to leave with people offering kind words. I went through the motions, taking pictures, smiling wide and agreeing with anything anyone said to me.

By the time we got to the car, I could feel my headache starting to return. I opened the door for Yuto like the good gentleman I had been taught to be before moving around to the other side. He chatted excitedly as we sat in a line of traffic before finally making it a few miles down the road to an ice cream shop.

I looked over his shoulder and saw him posting a few of the pictures on social media, reminding me that Barbara would skin me alive if I didn't post anything. I had silenced notifications on my phone because I had started getting so many alerts and texts.

"Oh my god, I've got to call my mom," I said, pulling out my wallet. "Get me whatever you get."

I pushed my card in Yuto's hands but he laughed.

"No way, this is on me. Our first of several celebrations."

Smiling, I turned my phone off airplane mode and immediately started getting text and voicemail alerts. One of them was from my mother.

"Mom?" I said when I heard the line click.

"Oh my god, Johnny, congratulations! I saw that you won. I'm so happy for you!"

I listened to her go on and on about how proud she was of me and watched the people walking outside, going about their lives like it was any other day. When Yuto appeared beside me, holding two ice cream sundaes, I knew it was time to extract myself from the conversation.

"I've got to go now, Mom. I love you. I love you, too. Okay. Bye."

I hung up and saw Yuto's wide grin as he offered one of the sundaes.

"Thank you."

We moved to a table and sat in silence as we took our first bites.

"Can we... talk about Jace?" he asked finally.

I nodded as I spooned a bite into my mouth.

"I think... maybe..."

"Go on," I said with a grin.

"I think you're holding on to this idea of him and it's hurting you."

"Okay."

"You're a good person," Yuto said, leaning over to put his hand on top of mine. "I think maybe you think you don't deserve the life you have. But you're a good human."

"Thanks," I said awkwardly, pulling my hand away.

He moved closer and tilted his head up, reaching in for my face. The instant his lips touched mine I felt my stomach twist into a one solid knot as my heart began to race. His hand slid to the back of my neck and the knot slowly started to dissolve bit by bit as I allowed myself to lean into him.

I pulled my lips back. "You're a good person too."

"I know," he said simply. His eyes glistened against the darkening sky.

"And a good kisser," I said without thinking.

He smiled and slipped his hand to my knee. "Yeah?"

"Yeah," I said, biting my lower lip and nodding.

"Hurry up and finish your ice cream," he instructed.

"Yes, sir," I complied.

SEASON 1 - EPISODE 12

Some Kind of Homage

I looked at my desk and made sure that everything was exactly where it was supposed to be. Pens, ready. Computer, plugged in. Bourbon, poured. I was as ready as I could be to begin working on the pilot I had been putting off for a full week.

Ext. Desert.

Dick:

Why are we in a desert?

Johnny:

What the fuck. What are you doing? You're not even a character here.

Dick:
I am now.

Johnny:
You're not.

(JOHNNY *deletes* DICK *from the manuscript. Only* DICK *doesn't listen. He reappears quickly despite* JOHNNY'S *frantic attempts to remove him from his life.*)

Dick:
Wow. Dick move.

Johnny:
Shut up.

(JESUS *is working on his carpentry in an open-air barn. He notices* JUDAS *standing against a beam, watching him.*)

Dick:
It's a wood joke, right? Jesus's wood?

Johnny:
No, god. How cheap...

Dick:
(snickers) You're working it out though, aren't you? Wood, dick, working on his wood. Working out his wood.

Johnny:

It's not funny. It's barely clever.

(*DICK laughs while JOHNNY wonders if the wood dick joke is worth pursuing. JOHNNY tries not to think too hard about the fact that he has used up several days of the three weeks he was given to write a script and absolutely refuses to acknowledge that while he should be writing the script, he's fucking around.*)

Jesus:
I can see you, you know.

Dick:
Are they speaking English? Aren't they like, not English?

Johnny:
What are you talking about?

Dick:
(*yelling*) Why are they British?!

Johnny:
WHO THE FUCK SAID THEY WERE BRITISH?!

Dick:
THEY ARE USING BRITISH ACCENTS.

Johnny:
IT'S FUCKING WORDS—THERE'S NO INTONATION GIVEN. SHUT THE FUCK UP.

Judas:
(*In a completely not British accent*) Sorry, master, I just—

Jesus:
Just what?

Dick:
What the fuck, is this porn? Are you writing Pedro Pascal Jesus porn? What the fuck is going through your mind? You wanna fuck Jesus? Or you wanna fuck Pedro?

Johnny:
I swear to Pedro Jesus, I will remove you from every memory on the planet. You will be a smudge in the history of bad animated late night television.

Dick:
An Emmy-winning smudge, you piece of shit. You think that scares me? I'm you. The only thing that scares me is failure. And being alone. Which you're really killing, by the way.

Johnny:
Jesus, fucking, Christ.

Dick:
Should there be commas there?

Johnny:
Now you're correcting my grammar? Are you fucking kidding me?

Dick:
(*laughs*)

Johnny:
(*JOHNNY grabs the nearest knife and stabs DICK*)

Dick:
Nice try…

(DICK *somehow evades the knife and is still alive. But he never was alive to begin with so there's really no way he can be alive still. JOHNNY begins to wonder if all it takes is for him to imagine that DICK is dead and see if maybe he would be dead.*)

(*Nothing happens.*)

Dick:
You can't get rid of me. You know what that would mean if you did.

Johnny:
What would that mean?

Dick:
That you're abandoning Jace. Moving on. Putting him in the past.

Johnny:
That's stupid. Eventually I am going to have to move on. Jace is dead. He *is* in the past. That's the whole point. He is now a fixed moment and I'm not. I'm not going to let him keep me from living.

(JOHNNY *realizes he's been afraid to say that for months. That by writing this work he thinks he is finally moving on. That he's doing this alone and for himself. Specifically something that* JACE *never thought was a good idea. He worries that by producing something on his own he'll forget what it was like to produce something with* JACE. *But the reality he's been avoiding is that he will never have the ability to create something with JACE again. And this weird psychological manifestation of JACE wasn't doing anything productive. It was just holding him back from moving on.)*

Dick:
Damn. That's cold, bro.

Johnny:
But true.

(JOHNNY understands he's arguing with himself and guesses that can't really be that healthy.)

Johnny:
Eventually, we're going to have to say goodbye.

Dick:
Yeah. Eventually.

Johnny:
Eventually.

13

As You Know, Bob...

I pulled at the tie around my neck, unsure if it was too much. I never wore ties. Jace would have shown up in a Hawaiian shirt or something to make it look like he wasn't taking it very seriously. A banana suit maybe? I could see him showing up to mediation in a banana suit.

I felt like I was going to throw up and honestly wondered if doing so would make me feel better. Each step to the courthouse felt longer and longer and when I reached the top, a familiar little duck appeared with both wings in the air like he was Rocky Balboa.

"Would you stop that?" I whispered.

I followed instructions as I made my way through security, knowing I wasn't going to get a gold star for not being flagged. Dick thought otherwise and was trying to pants the security guard, despite only reaching his knees.

Bruce had advised me not to come, but I felt like I had to

see Hansome face to face. Riley had already told me she wouldn't be there. I hit the elevator button and waited.

"Johnny?"

I turned to see Hansome standing there awkwardly.

"Oh, god, hi."

"I didn't think..." he started before stopping himself.

Didn't think I'd show up, I almost finished for him but didn't.

He licked his lips like he was about to start speaking but stopped. "We probably shouldn't be talking here."

"Yeah," I agreed. "But, I mean, it's good to see you again."

"Yeah, same to you. Listen," he started, "I'm sorry about Jace. I didn't mean to dump more..."

I wondered if he was feeling guilt over Jace's death and if he knew he couldn't admit that to me here.

"If you get him to admit it, they will put him away for life," Dick quacked.

It's not a trial, I reminded Dick, *and he's not being judged. Dumbass.*

"I get it," I said as the elevator ding signaled its arrival.

We rode in silence, shuffling as others joined until we got to our floor. When the door opened and I exited, I saw Bruce standing there, waiting. He looked from me to Hansome, eyes wide.

"Did you talk to him?"

"No. I did good," I said, shoving my hands in my pockets.

Hansome had moved to his lawyer and they were in a similarly quiet conversation opposite us. It was uncomfortable, knowing we were enemies, but also knowing because it was something wrong that I had done. I knew I wasn't the one who took his art, or recreated it, but I was responsible for it and the person who had done it.

I had never been close to him, but I certainly never wanted to hurt him, or anyone.

"What's our strategy?" Dick asked Bruce, crossing his wings angrily.

Bruce ran through the outcomes both desired and undesired. What would happen if we couldn't settle, if we had to go to trial, if we had to add him to the copyright, if we had to go higher than we were willing to go, if we had to do this and that. I didn't really care, honestly, I just wanted to get it over with.

The fear of losing *Dick* was gone. I had already lost him. The show and the creation could never be the same for me ever again and I knew I was going to have to let him go soon. Was that shitty of me to care less because of what had happened? Would I have been able to handle it if this was happening with Jace present?

I wondered what he would have done.

Did he give up because of this? Did he give up because of Riley? Was it me? How did I still not know?

We all moved into the little conference room and the two camps set up opposite one another. Hansome avoided making eye contact with me and that was fine. I was too distracted by Dick drawing penises on the whiteboard behind them.

"We have evidence to show that my client paid the claimant for his idea when this was originally brought up. As you know, if money exchanged hands for the idea, then your client would have no claim at this time to the damages he's seeking. And *Dick* would be the legal property of my client."

Hansome's lawyer turned to him quickly and asked the mediator for a moment of privacy. The mediator pointed to a smaller room at the back of the tiny room we were in.

"Is that..." I started, but was cut off by Bruce who raised his hand quickly to make me stop.

I wanted to ask if it was true that Jace had paid Hansome for the idea. I didn't know what to believe. I certainly wouldn't put it past Jace to do either. There was a version of him in my mind where he did steal the idea from Hansome, knowing he could talk himself out of it if it ever came to that. The other side of him gave Hansome a wad of cash and had him sign something, knowing that was all he would need to prove he owned it after all.

Hansome and his stuffy lawyer returned and stood behind the table. I guessed that their refusal to sit was a good sign.

"In light of this new evidence, my client has offered to withdraw their claim. We will no longer be seeking damages."

Bruce grinned and slid a piece of paper across the table. "We were hoping you'd say that. According to paperwork I have from my client, I would still like to offer this sum as settlement. To ensure that this issue is never brought forward again."

I watched Hansome's lawyer nod in his direction before Hansome reached forward and signed the paper.

"That's it?" Dick cried. "I thought there was going to be some kind of battle or turf war. Something? That was fucking anticlimactic as hell. Are you trying to bore the audience?"

I fought the urge to shrug to the figment of my imagination glaring at me from across the room. If it was truly over, I would be thrilled. Nothing about any of this was enjoyable.

Even in death, Jace got his way. There wasn't a situation I had seen where he didn't get exactly what he wanted, every fucking time. It was the kind of thing that should have been studied. *Every. Fucking. Time.*

"Will you please eat some fucking food?" Jace asked, pushing forward his bag of popcorn next to me at the table.

"I eat food."

"You don't, actually, and you think no one will notice."

I rolled my eyes and shuffled the pile of headshots in front of me.

"Who is next?"

"Martin Bedford."

"Send him in."

I stopped my shuffling to look up at Jace. "We're waiting on Kate."

Jace groaned loudly and slid down in his chair.

"You don't have to be here. I can do this by myself," I proposed.

"Fuck off. You won't choose the right one. You think everyone is good."

"So far, everyone *has* been good."

"Oh my god," Jace yelled. "Tell me you're joking. Please tell me you're joking."

He stood up and started wandering around the empty room.

"What are you doing?"

"Maybe I'm next. Maybe I should audition."

I shook my head and grabbed a handful of his popcorn. "Absolutely not."

"Why? I can do it. And better than these assholes. They don't even understand Dick. I get him on a micro-level."

"I don't know what that means," I said, exasperated, "but really, no, you're going to be busy enough as it is. You're writing, animating, running a production company, you don't need to be voicing a character too."

"I'm barely animating, you're actually writing and let's be honest, I don't do a fucking thing at our company. This will save you money?"

He always knew exactly where to hit me. I threw a piece of popcorn at him. "Fuck off."

Laughing loudly, he moved back and opened his mouth expectantly before shifting his hands quickly as though trying to push me back from across the room. "Okay, okay, wait, if I catch it in my mouth I get to voice the character."

I raised an eyebrow, debating it. He knew he was close to winning me over.

"I only get three chances," he negotiated before scooting backwards a few steps, "and I'll start here."

Grinning, I nodded. "Deal."

"Okay, great," he cried, clapping a few times as he lowered himself into a squat to get ready.

"What the fuck are you doing?" I laughed.

"Just limbering up." He shifted side to side on his knees rapidly, watching me as he did. "I've got to be limber."

"Enough. I think you're plenty limber."

"Alright, alright, alright," he clapped again and raised both hands in front of him as though preparing to catch a football. "And you have to be serious, you can't be stupid with it."

"I know. I will."

I pushed my chair back from the table and leaned forward to get the best balance I could. "This one is just a test. So I can see my arm."

"Perfect," he agreed, nodding vigorously.

I threw the popcorn with as much earnestness as I could and watched it zoom past his open mouth.

"Okay, too much juice."

"Alright. Calibrated?" he asked, resuming his previous position.

"Yeah, I think so."

He nodded and prepared himself. The first throw hit his face and bounced off, rolling on the carpet.

"Second chance."

He clapped and I could see him putting all his focus into the moment.

I let the piece of popcorn leave my hand and it flew directly into his mouth. Before I knew what was happening, he took off, running frantically in circles around the room screaming and clapping as he did. When his victory lap reached me, he stuck his tongue out so I could see pieces of chewed popcorn on it.

"I can see that, you gross shit," I said with a smile. "You win."

"I'm fucking Dick, baby! I'm fucking Dick!"

Kate entered the room and watched Jace run in circles, screaming.

"What did I miss?"

"I think we're done auditioning for today," I said, shuffling the papers in front of me, unable to conceal my smile.

Jace galloped close to Kate and pulled her by the hands, turning her around and around as he did. She giggled as her blonde hair bounced around her shoulders. She and Jace circled once more before he stopped and dipped her in front of the table.

"What is going on?" she asked amidst her little laugh, pulling away from Jace to look at me.

"He's celebrating," I explained, reaching for another handful of popcorn. "He cast himself as Dick."

"Oh," she said, sobering up. "There's a room of people out there. Want me to dismiss them?"

I nodded, collecting my things. "Thanks, Kate."

She turned and headed for the door and I watched her leave, waiting until the door clicked shut to continue. "It's a terrible idea, you know."

Jace had stopped running and was standing in the middle of the room, his hair flopped across his forehead and hands hooked on his hips as he caught his breath. "What? That?" he asked, pointing to the door. "That's not an idea, trust me."

I leveled a stare at him. "Voicing Dick. You're going to be too busy."

"No, *you* think it's a bad idea. Because you don't think I'll stick around, don't you?"

"That's a dumb thing to say." *Out loud*—I wanted to add, but didn't.

Jace laughed and came over to the table, climbing up enough to sit on top and reach over to grab the bag of popcorn. He shoved a handful in his mouth before talking. "Just admit it. That's what you're thinking."

"That wasn't what I was thinking."

"Well, bad news, buddy, you're stuck with me now." He reached over and slapped my shoulder a few times as he said it. "You should look at it this way—me being the voice means I can't leave. Ever think of that? You can't get rid of me now, even if you wanted to."

I smiled, but wasn't sure if he saw any humor in it. The reality was it was the most transparent admission he had ever made that he was desperate to have a reason to be needed and it made me sad inside. For all his faults, he was so very fragile.

"You know that's the last thing I want," I said sarcastically. I pushed the nearly empty bag toward him before standing. "I'm done."

He picked it up and slid off the edge of the table. "What are you doing now? We had this blocked off until three, right?"

"Yeah."

"Riley and I are going to this exhibit thing out at Getty tonight. Do you want to go with us?"

"What is it?"

"Fuck if I know," Jace said, emptying the bag into his mouth. "Her idea. Want me to ask her?"

I shook my head. "No, thanks. I'm pretty tired. I'll see you tomorrow."

"Alright," he said behind me as I walked to the door. "Invitation's always open. You know that."

"I know!" I called, raising my empty hand before pushing against the office door.

It *was* a terrible idea. I knew it then as much as I knew it now. And there was a part of me that would never not wonder if Jace thought about that very conversation before he stuck a pistol in his mouth and pulled the trigger.

———

My phone was buzzing in my hand, though it took me a minute to register it. I read the name: *Riley*.

"Hello?"

"Hey," she said, her voice flat.

"What's wrong?" I asked, suddenly concerned.

"They are installing Jace's headstone today. I thought you should be there."

"Oh," I paused. "Yeah, thanks. I'll be there. Unless you don't want me there?"

She sighed. "No, I want you there. Be there at eleven."

"Great. Thanks."

"See you soon."

The line went dead and I looked up at the clock. I needed to get up and get dressed. I had been sitting in my living room for the past three hours, staring at the wall. Moving to the bedroom, I pulled on a nicer shirt, slacks and debated a suit jacket. It seemed like kind of a formal thing, even if it would just be me and Riley. Jace would have hated us in formal clothes.

I pulled the jacket on and slipped into my shoes before heading to the door, patting my pockets for phone and keys.

"Where are we going?" Dick asked at the door.

"Cemetery."

"Again? For what? Did you kill someone else?"

"I didn't kill anyone," I said, exasperated, as I locked the door and headed to my car.

"Then what are we doing at the cemetery?"

"Haven't we established that you know what I'm thinking already? Why am I still explaining things to you?"

"Uh oh," he said, "continuity error? That's not a good sign, buddy, that means a new writer has taken over."

"There are no writers. This is real life. Why the fuck am I explaining again?"

We climbed into the car and as soon as I could, I queued up my Eminem. It seemed to be one of the only things that made Dick either disappear or quiet down. I guessed it had something to do with the loud beats preventing me from hearing myself think.

As soon as I got to the graveyard and stopped the car, Dick appeared out of the corner of my eye.

"It looks different."

I looked around. He was right, though not in the sense that anything had changed, really, that the passage of time felt evident from the last time we were here and I didn't want to acknowledge it.

"Can't I do this on my own?" I asked quietly.

"We're not alone. Riley's here." Dick pointed at Jace's car sitting along the paved roadway.

"Yeah," I said as I opened the car door. "That's true."

We walked slowly up to where she was standing, looking carefully at the stone in front of her.

It was shiny, that was nice.

Jason Thomas Van Noy

(1986-2022)

It was strange, seeing his life contained to such a small little thing on this Earth. He used to always joke about how stupid cemeteries were and how odd it was that we attempted to hold on to pieces of the dead. I had no way to explain to him now that the pieces weren't for the dead, but for the living.

I moved closer and brushed away a few specks of dirt before reaching into my pocket and pulling out one of our little miniature yellow glass ducks. I set it carefully on the little ledge at the end of the stone, right under the 2022. It was smaller than the final digit that signaled the end of his life.

"It's so weird," I said. I didn't know what else to say.

"I'm actually relieved," Riley replied, in tears. "I don't know how much more I can take."

I turned to her, watching the tears welling up. I didn't cry when Jace died. I hadn't cried about any of it. It was too sad to make me cry. Instead, I had been numb, stumbling around, observing it all without participating. But here, seeing her cry, feeling the raw pain she allowed to leave her body, shook me more than the death itself.

"I'm so sorry," I heard myself repeating. I'm sorry. I *was* sorry. I was so sorry.

"It's okay," she said, moving closer to me and wrapping her arms around herself. "We're going to be okay."

I didn't know if I believed her.

"There's something I need to share with you."

I pulled back from her and ran my fingers over my chin. "What?"

"You asked after it all happened if there was a note and I told you there wasn't. Which, there wasn't, really, but he did leave me a voicemail. Before. If you want to hear it, I'll play it for you."

Shaking my head, I stepped back. I wasn't sure if I wanted

to. Every new piece of information was sending me deeper into this unknown hole of misery and how could this voicemail offer any kind of closure?

"I don't know."

"I'm going to delete it. I can't have it on my phone anymore. But I wanted to give you the opportunity to hear it before I did."

"Did it help?"

She shook her head.

"Go ahead."

She pulled the phone out of her purse and clicked through the sequence to get to the voicemail. Once it started playing she put it on speaker. The minute I heard Jace's voice my heart felt like it dropped to my feet. It wasn't like Dick—hearing Dick was jarring, but it was a memory—a soundboard of pieces of Jace that I had collected over the years. This... this was actually him.

"Hey, Riles," it started. "I wanted to leave this for you. Like, I don't know, like to try and explain. I know there's no explanation. I know that you won't accept anything I say now. I think if I could explain it, I wouldn't be here. Uh, listen, I'm sorry. I'm sorry for everything I've put you through and everything I'm about to. You deserve so much more. But I can't be here anymore. I need to go somewhere that doesn't expect anything from me. Once I'm gone, you'll need Johnny—he can help you. He's good like that. I love you—more than I even understand. And I'm so sorry for this. I'm just... I'll see you someday soon. I love you."

His voice had broken and gotten so quiet in the end that I barely heard the last *I love you*. The last words she had from Jace were, *I love you*.

"Jesus."

Riley had begun silently crying again and pushed a tissue across her face before lowering the phone.

"I don't think I can keep this with me. I have to delete it."

"Yeah. That makes sense."

"I know that he loved me. I know that. But I can't reconcile those two people in my mind. If he loved me, like he said he did, he wouldn't have done that to me. And he wouldn't have kept the lawsuit from me. And he would have just told me what was crushing him. And he wouldn't have written those things about me. It doesn't even make sense to me that those two people could both be Jace."

"Yeah."

I shoved my hands into my pockets, unsure of what else to say.

"Did he leave you a voicemail?"

I shook my head.

"What were his last words to you? Do you remember?"

I did.

But I shook my head again instead.

"That's not true. Why are you lying? Please stop lying to me."

"You look tired as shit," I said.

"What the hell, Johnny."

"Those were Jace's final words to me."

She watched me carefully as though trying to decipher a code in the message.

"He went to see you, didn't he? I remember the night before he said he was going to see you about something."

"Yeah," I admitted, looking down at the headstone. "He came over that night."

"So, what happened?" she asked, looking me in the eyes.

"Nothing happened."

But we both knew it was a lie.

TEN WEEKS EARLIER

The knocking from the door came in a rapid succession—as though the person outside was trying to escape from something chasing them.

I moved a little closer, trying to listen for any indication of who it might be.

"Johnny!" Jace yelled on the other side. "Let me in!"

Startled, I pulled the door open to see what was going on. "What the hell are you doing?"

He hadn't told me he was coming over, which he normally did if it wasn't a previously scheduled visit.

"Can I come in?" he asked, frantically.

Still confused, I moved back to allow him the space to enter, which he did by practically shoving me to the side. Once in the living room, he began pacing around in wide circles uncontrollably.

"What is your problem?" I asked.

Jace continued pacing in front of me, circle after circle like a tiger in a pen too small for its size.

"Nothing is the problem. I'm great, John. Can't you tell? Can't you see how great I am?"

"You're freaking me out."

Jace laughed and paced and laughed and paced.

"Sit down at least."

He did and pulled out a cigarette.

"Seriously?"

"What? Fuck, can I not fucking smoke in here? You used to smoke too, you know. Until you became an old faggot."

It was meant to hurt, but it didn't.

"Is Blake here?"

I leaned back in the chair, unsure of what to do. This felt a little different than normal. "No. Blake's not here."

"You two break up yet?"

"No."

"Let me know when you do." He lit the cigarette.

He smoked like it was the only thing keeping him alive.

"Are you using?"

"The fuck, man. What kind of question is that?"

"The kind you're refusing to answer?"

"I'm not fucking using. Jesus."

I pulled my leg over the other. "What's going on with you? Is something wrong?"

He laughed a sad laugh that made me uncomfortable. Like he was laughing at a joke that only he would understand.

"What's funny about that?"

"I don't think..." he cut himself off and took a long draw on his cigarette. "Are you happy?"

I slid down further in my chair. "What? Like right now or in general?"

"In general."

"Sure, I guess. We have fun."

"Do we though?" He leaned forward on his knees. "We did, sure, but now we just sit in rooms regurgitating bad ideas that someone else draws up and prints on t-shirts. Is that what we wanted?"

I didn't know what to say. I had never wanted that. I only wanted to create shit. But Jace never settled for anything but the most.

"Money's good."

He laughed again. "Sure, Johnny, the money is great. But it's more things to make more money and when you have more money you have to make more things to make more money and all we do is make to make and make to make without ever thinking about why we're creating. I don't even want to create anymore. Do you? Really?"

"I don't know," I admitted. "I still enjoy it, I think. All I know is writing. What is this? Where is it coming from?"

"It means nothing. Don't you see? The work and the time all put toward nothing. It means absolutely nothing."

I didn't think that was true. "So, what? You're saying we quit?"

"No. We do nothing. That's the beauty of it all. We could do nothing and it will still continue. It's all happening without us being involved." His voice fell to barely above a whisper. "We were never needed to begin with."

His eyes looked down at his interlocked fingers and held a kind of sadness that I couldn't understand.

"I think you're just tired. You need to get some sleep. Have you eaten any food today? I can make you something real quick if you want."

"Yeah, no," he said, standing and taking a quick draw on the cigarette. "You're probably right. I'm tired."

"Get some sleep, please. And eat some protein."

"I will. I didn't mean it when I called you a faggot."

"I know, Jace."

"We're like two pieces of a whole, aren't we? Together? Like we make each other whole?"

That little voice of dread returned. It wasn't like him to be sentimental.

"Sure. I think so."

"I really lucked out by finding you."

"Thanks, man. You too."

"You made me a better writer."

I moved close enough to slap him on the back. "What is this? Why are you being all sappy? That's pretty gay of you."

I expected at least a little laugh, but I didn't get one. He looked at me as though he was looking through me, as though I no longer existed to him.

"Just getting old, I guess. The older I get, the more I remember what it was like before I was told who I was supposed to be sometimes. It feels like a different person completely. You ever feel that way?"

"All the time." I admitted, pushing my hands into my pockets.

"I brought something for you," he said suddenly, bounding out of the front door.

I moved near the door and watched him pull a box from the backseat of his car.

"What's this?" I asked, accepting the box.

"Just some of our old shit. I was cleaning things out and thought you might want it."

"What for?"

He shrugged and moved back a little. "Just if you wanted. If not, you can toss it."

I looked inside and saw the top layer of his drawings—some going back as far as college. "Why would you get rid of these?"

"Just cleaning out the past I guess." He smiled as he lit another cigarette. "It's kind of fun, going back through it. Reliving the good old days. Those were fun times."

I nodded, starting to understand the box for what it was. I put the box down on the steps. "Are you finally breaking up with me?"

He smiled and put the cigarette gently between my lips. "It's okay."

"Is it?" I asked, removing the cigarette.

"Yeah. I'm not upset about that part of it. But I do worry. About Riley. And you."

"Well, what if I said I can't go on without you? That you have to stay here to help us. What would you say then?"

"I'd ask you not to make me go through this any more."

"You know I can't let you do this. We'll get you help," I said quietly.

"I'm so tired, John." His voice was breaking with each word. "I'm just so tired. It's all pain. Please, let me have this little bit of control over my own life. It's the only thing I have left."

I cleared my throat as I felt it closing up. "Please let me help you."

He laughed his little laugh as he shook his head before moving forward to grab onto me. "You have no idea how much you've helped me. You've always helped me. We'll find each other later, remember? I promised."

"So, I guess this is goo—"

"Shh, shh," he cut me off. "None of that."

His hand reached up and held my head at the base of my neck. The touch of his hands against my skin sent me into a sob I hadn't expected. "Just stay here. Just stay with me. You can sleep in the guest room or on the couch even. Don't leave this house, okay?"

"We both know that's not how it works. I stay here tonight, I leave you the next night. I stay another night, I find a way the week after that. I'm not leaving you tonight; don't call the cops on me or anything. But I am letting you know that this is what the future will be. It's not your decision. This is my life. And I want to have a say in letting myself have some peace. I'll say good-bye before it's all said and done. Trust me, you can't get rid of me that easily." He pulled back and gave me a long kiss on my forehead.

"Fuck you."

Laughing, he pulled back and took the cigarette from my hand. He bounced down the stairs and moved backwards toward his car. "Thank you. You have no idea how much I owe you. Please get some sleep. You look tired as shit."

He smiled and it was the happiest I had seen him in a very long time. I could feel tears on my face.

"Fuck the absolute shit out of you."

He laughed loudly as he held two fingers up in a peace sign before getting in the car and backing slowly out of the driveway. I raised my hand in goodbye as I watched him leave.

He killed himself the next day.

14

Red Herring

My phone buzzed on the table and I leaned forward to see who it was. Yuto. I hesitated a brief moment before answering.

"What's up?"

"What are you doing tonight?" he asked.

I knew the answer was nothing, but I wasn't sure if I wanted to agree to anything with him before knowing what it was.

"I don't know. What's up?" I asked again.

"Come to yoga with me."

"What?"

"Yoga. I go to a class every week and you'd be amazed how much it helps your soul."

"I doubt that."

"Just try it. Worst case scenario, you find out you don't like yoga."

I smiled. "True."

"Come on. I have a guest pass so it won't cost you anything. Try it and see."

"Alright," I conceded. "When is it?"

He shared the time and location before hanging up. As soon as the call was over, I realized I'd forgotten to ask what I was supposed to wear. I guessed gym shorts and was glad that earlier in the year I had made some half-assed commitment to trying to be more physically active. The resolution had only really resulted in me buying the clothes, going running once, and then promptly giving up.

"You look ridiculous," Dick said as he looked me up and down in my shorts.

"Shut up," I sighed as I sat to tie my tennis shoes.

"Don't you feel ridiculous? If you don't feel absolutely stupid in that, I don't know what else I can do to help you."

"I guess that's it then. I'm going to head out since you can't help me."

"Let me in, Johnny!" I heard Dick yelling as I shut the door.

Yuto smiled wide when I walked in the gym. The smell of sweat and the air fresheners used to cover the sweat hit me in a wave as I approached.

"I'm so glad you showed up."

"You thought I'd bail?" I asked with a smile.

"I wouldn't blame you if you did. But I'm really glad you didn't."

It got quiet between us, the noise of the gym filling the gap. I looked at the front desk. "So, what do I need to do here?"

"Oh, right. I think I can sign you in and then you can put your stuff up in the locker."

He spoke with the person at the front desk, who was far too chipper for her own good. She and Yuto chatted easily as I stood awkwardly next to him. I wondered if he had ever met a stranger. Every person was an opportunity to him. A chance to experience more of humanity and learn. It had to be exhausting.

"Thanks Hailey," he said, tapping the top of the counter as he moved away. "You're all set."

I didn't say anything but could feel the smile at the corner of my mouth.

"What?" he asked, grinning wide.

"Nothing. Let's get this over with."

"Who knows, you might like it."

The studio room was filled with people already stretching on their little foam mats. The walls at the front and far right side were completely made of mirrors and I caught a glimpse of myself as I followed Yuto to pick up a mat. Dick was right, I did look ridiculous.

The instructor had long curly hair pulled back into a ponytail and greeted us warmly as we arranged our mats on the floor. I sat and crossed my legs like the rest of the group, waiting for the class to start.

Yuto made it look so easy. His normally cheerful face was set in a stone of peaceful unity. Slowly he lifted one arm up to the ceiling and balanced everything in his body and mind all at the same time.

The instructor called out the step-by-step instructions for each pose and I was too focused on getting them completed correctly to allow myself any room for healing breaths or meditation.

"What color is your breath right now?" the instructor asked as he folded himself at the front of the room.

What the hell kind of question is that? I wondered as I looked to Yuto. Despite his closed eyes, his mouth finally curled into a slight smile.

I knew there was no way that kind of statement went past him without the slightest bit of amusement.

"Focus now on your breathing," the teacher said from his pedestal. "Breathe only with your right lung."

My eyes darted uncontrollably to Yuto who had his head bent over his shoulder. His eyes met mine and I saw his shoulders shake with concealed laughter. I wondered if he was only laughing with his right lung.

I tried to focus on releasing all of my blue air as I held my left leg out as far as it would go. Cheating a little, I started to pull it back toward my body as slowly as I could before the instructor announced it.

"Slowly roll yourself back."

I watched the girl to my right inch further and further back until she flattened herself like a tortilla against the ground. It was impressive to see someone have so much control over every tiny muscle in their body.

"Now feel your body telling you what it needs. Breathe in to ground yourself to the earth below you. Feel the energy coming and going through your soul."

I spread my arms out next to me and fixed my eyes to a metal joint in the ceiling. This part with the lights off and the quiet tonal sounds of tranquility was nice. I tried to feel as much as I could feel, but that collectively amounted to not that much.

"This pose is called corpse pose."

Which was fine.

"We're winding down and allowing everything to leave our body that we no longer need."

Totally fine.

"Breathe out what you wish to expel. This idea of rebirth really is just us choosing to let go and become who we know we are. You can be reborn every minute of every day. You can die and renew as much as you want and should. Open yourself to the grounding of the earth and allow that energy to make you reborn."

I can die and be reborn. I can die. I can.

I closed my eyes and wished for the comfort of rebirth. I exhaled as much of the death that had taken over my life and prayed for the renewal of spirit. Once all the air was out, I held my breath, terrified that breathing would now allow more bad to come in.

Rebirth—daily.

Death—and rebirth.

The pressure in my chest grew and I reached my hands up to grab where it hurt. I still couldn't breathe. *Don't let it in.*

My knees pulled themselves into my body, now every piece of me attempting to calm and comfort my brain.

"Johnny," I heard from a distance. "Johnny, are you okay?"

I opened my eyes and inhaled a deep breath while looking into the concerned eyes of Yuto, watching me from above in the dim light.

"Are you okay?" he asked again.

I felt the warmth of the tears running down my face before nodding slowly. "Yeah. I think so."

When I sat up, I was conscious for the first time that everyone in the class was watching us.

"I'm sorry," I said quickly, standing up. I could hear him rushing after me as I left the room.

"I'm sorry," he said, gently touching my arm. "That was a lot."

I pulled back reflexively, before realizing I did. "I'm fine. I'm fine."

His lips drew into a sympathetic line and he shuffled forward a little. "It's okay to not be okay. You know that, right?"

I nodded.

"What do you need?"

"I don't know." I admitted. "I honestly don't know anymore."

Frantically, I wiped at my eyes, annoyed that I felt stupid for letting a room full of strangers see me cry.

"Want to go sit in the sauna?"

I nodded again.

"Come on."

He took my hand gently and led me back to the locker room where the entrance to the sauna was.

"Why don't you get towels and go ahead and go back there? I'll be right there."

I don't know why, but I felt like I couldn't speak and nodded as he walked back to the studio. I imagined him apologizing to the instructor for my insane behavior and felt that familiar pit of embarrassment in knowing he would have to make excuses for me.

The tears renewed themselves out of sheer anger and I shuffled quickly to the water fountain to get a drink. My throat was starting to feel like it was closing and I needed air. The water helped, and by the time he got back I had stopped crying and was starting to calm down.

"I'm so sorry," I started, wrapping my hands around my elbows. "I didn't mean to embarrass you."

Yuto's face drew up in confusion. "Oh god, no, you didn't embarrass me. I'm the one that should be apologizing to you. That was intense. And you told me you weren't sure about it."

He stepped forward and put both of his hands over mine that were still gripping my arms tightly. "Are you okay?"

I nodded. The touch of his hands turned the knot into sand as it trickled out particle by particle.

"Come on," he urged, pulling me forward.

We grabbed towels and we went to the locker to change out of our clothes. There was an older man in the sauna with a towel draped over his head. Yuto and I sat on one of the benches and the heat on my bare skin felt nice.

"I had a panic attack in Whole Foods," he said out of nowhere.

"What?"

"A month after Eva died. I was shopping in Whole Foods and feeling really good about myself. I had gotten up, showered, dressed and drove myself to the store. I was nailing it. And then, suddenly, I saw bananas."

"Bananas?"

He laughed a small and sad laugh. "Yeah, bananas."

"Was it connected to something with you and Eva?"

"That's what's so funny. I can't think of a single inside joke or mental connection between my dead wife and a bundle of delicious yellow bananas. But I stopped when I saw them, sitting there, waiting to be picked, and it was like a switch just flipped."

I shifted my legs uncomfortably and pulled my towel tighter. "What happened?"

"I wound up on the floor. Like completely messed up. Eventually they called an ambulance because I'm sure they were scared or thought I was on drugs maybe. The EMT that took my pulse took the time to calm me down and ask some questions. It didn't take much to get my story out."

"Why are you telling me this?" I asked after a minute of silence.

"Just so you know that it really is okay to not be okay. No one else has to feel what you're feeling day in and day out. They might stare, feel uncomfortable or even judge, but it doesn't matter in the end. They don't know what it's like."

I used the edge of my towel to wipe my forehead that was already dripping in sweat.

"Can I say something that might hurt a little? If I'm crossing a line, you can tell me."

I wasn't sure where he was going with this. "I guess."

"I know I didn't know Jace. And I know I don't even know you, really, but I think you're holding on to an idealized version of what he was. And I think maybe he wasn't really that good for you. I think he used you in a lot of ways and you're too good of a person to make it an issue. I'm not trying to say anything bad about Jace, but I think you're holding onto an idea and it's not... really..." he struggled for the words, "healthy?"

"You didn't know him," I said, trying not to sound as angry as I felt.

"I know. I just... I worry, maybe, that you're holding on to this guilt about him? And I think maybe sometimes he made you feel bad about yourself? Someone can love you and still hurt you. In fact, those that love you can hurt you the most."

"Jace never hurt me," I said quietly before adding, "honestly, we hurt each other, I guess."

"I get it. If you're holding on to that for now to survive, then that's totally valid. You've got to do what you need to do right now. But if you're holding on to it to idolize him into something he wasn't, like you still feel the need to defend him or something, you don't have to do that. That's not your job anymore. And it shouldn't have been your job then either."

The bundle of anger that formed while he was talking loosened a little. He wasn't completely wrong that I spent so much of my time defending Jace to those around us, even when he didn't ask for it. I did feel like it was my responsibility for some reason.

"Why did I feel that?"

"Feel what?" Yuto asked.

"Responsible for him and everything he did?"

"Because you loved him. And he needed you. Some people need a little more help than others. And sometimes those people that need help find someone who is willing to help them. But the problem is a lot of times those people will use and use and use until there's nothing left to give."

"Yeah," I admitted. *Use and abuse.* "So are you a giver or a taker?"

He smiled. "I think I was a giver early in my life. I've gotten better though. And I think now I can see that in healthy relationships you have to switch off sometimes. It has to be both give and take every now and then."

"Hmm."

We paused as someone else entered the sauna and we all gave the polite nod before he continued.

"Can you imagine being with someone who took care of you when you needed it?"

"Yeah, that would be nice," I said, rubbing my towel over my face again.

Jace said he didn't know what it felt like to be in love. I knew all too well what that felt like. But I guessed it was time to admit to myself that I didn't really know what it meant to *be loved.*

I still believed that Jace loved me as much as he could. I think he struggled with affection and vulnerability of any kind and it did comfort me some to know that the closest he ever got was between us. I couldn't have asked for anything else from him. But in the end it was never going to be enough for me.

And it apparently wasn't enough for Riley either.

"So how do I get rid of that? Like purging him from my system?"

"I don't know that you can, really. I think it will get easier for you, over time. It's not the same, but I had a really hard time opening back up after Eva died. I think in some ways I thought I would never love anyone else ever again."

Though I wasn't really ready to admit that, I had a sneaking feeling that I was telling myself that was the case for myself with Jace. That maybe he was the long-lost love of my life who I'd never be able to have for my own. And I had to let that go.

"That's not true though."

"Yeah," he said with a grin, "I know that now. I think she'd be okay with me these days. And maybe that's bullshit I tell myself to feel better. Honestly? That's allowed too."

I laughed. "Good to know."

We settled into a silence as I built up the courage to ask another question. "If you could have stopped Eva's suffering, like taken her pain away, would you have?"

"One hundred percent," he answered without hesitation. "I would have done anything to take that away from her. She didn't deserve a slow death."

"But what about the hope that she would have gotten better? Like beaten it?"

He paused. "Do you want me to answer for Eva or Jace? Because I'm guessing we're talking about Jace here. You could have found him every time in every scenario. You could have pulled him out of his darkness and drug him back to reality and even taken any dangerous object around him. You could have saved him every time and still lost him. His life was never yours to lose. You have to see that."

I wasn't sure if I was able to accept that.

"Did you like the actual yoga part?"

"Aside from the panic attack? No. Not really."

His laugh caught in his throat as he tried not to be too loud for the benefit of the other two men present.

"Thank you for inviting me, but I'm for sure never going to yoga again with you."

Yuto laughed loudly. "Never say never, Johnny."

We sat in the steam and the silence and it was nice.

"Were you in love with Jace?" he asked after a minute.

"Yeah," I admitted, "I really, really was."

He reached over from the bench and gave my hand a squeeze.

15

The water lapped against the sand in front of me and it made me angry. Day by day it felt like I was starting to hate the ocean more. The ocean was supposed to be tranquil. It calmed some people. But now, I hated it.

I woke up to someone shaking my shoulder with minimal effort.

"What?" I asked, still groggy.

"Your phone keeps ringing," Blake replied in the darkness.

"What?"

Rolling over, I reached for the phone and the screen lit up in the darkness. I had five missed calls from Riley. "Shit."

I pulled the charging cable out and headed to the bathroom.

"What is it?" Blake asked, watching me from the bed.

"I don't know. Riley?" I said quickly, as I shut the bathroom door and turned on the light, wincing momentarily at the brightness before calling her back.

"Johnny," she started. "Is Jace with you?"

"What?" I asked for the third time in a matter of seconds. "I'm home, asleep. What's going on?"

"He hasn't come home and I can't get ahold of him. It's unlike him. Did he say anything to you? Text you?"

"No, I don't think so. Hold on. Let me try to call him and I'll call you right back."

I pulled the phone away from my ear and swiped through to see if I had any texts or missed calls. They were all from Riley. I pushed the buttons to pull up my recent calls and clicked his name.

All I heard was a ringing noise as I looked at myself in the bathroom mirror. My hair was piled on one side and sticking up in the back. I let it ring a few more times before lowering the phone. If he wasn't answering Riley it was unlikely he would answer me. I texted him a quick message asking him to call before calling Riley back.

"Anything?"

"No," I admitted. "If he's seen the calls and texts and hasn't answered then maybe his phone is dead. He wouldn't ignore you."

"Yeah," she said as though she wasn't really sure. "What should I do?"

"Stay home. That's where he'll end up, I bet. Let me go check a few places and I'll let you know. Maybe he had a few drinks and passed out in his car or something. As soon as I find anything I'll call you. I'm sure he's fine. It's going to be fine."

"Thank you, Johnny," she said before hanging up.

I splashed some water on my face and brushed my teeth before heading back into the room to put some clothes on. There were only a few places that were options for where he might be hanging out. It was likely he was drunk somewhere. My thoughts were interrupted by the movement of Blake sitting up in the bed. The light from the bathroom illuminated our space enough for me to see the confusion on his face.

"What are you doing?" he asked, eyeing me as I slipped on a pair of pants. "What's the problem?"

"Jace is MIA."

"And?"

"I'm going to go look for him."

"At 2 o'clock in the morning?" Blake asked in disbelief.

"Yeah, she can't find him. He might be in trouble. Maybe I should call hospitals?"

"Why is Jace your responsibility?"

"I don't appreciate the tone," I huffed as I pulled on a shirt.

"You're really going to go out driving the streets of L.A. in the middle of the night looking for a grown man? What the fuck, Johnny. He's not *your* husband."

I stopped mid shoe thrust and turned to him. "What?"

"It's always like this, isn't it? Jace needs help and you drop everything to run to his side. He and Riley get in a fight and you play mediator to their batshit drama. He goes off the deep end and you're willing to drown trying to get to where he is. Why is it always him first? Why is *he* the most important person in your life? Can you explain that to your boyfriend?"

"I can't do this right now," I said, pulling on my other shoe.

"Can't or won't?"

"What is the problem here? You want me to just ignore him?"

"I want you to admit that he's your priority in life. Your only priority, really."

Angrily, I grabbed the hoodie draped over my desk chair and turned to face Blake directly. "You're right. He is first because he came first. He's closer to me than my own family and I'm not going to let you make me feel bad about that. If he's in my life, you're going to have to make space for him."

"And if I asked you not to be friends with him?"

I shook my head admitting to myself for the first time what that meant.

"Wow," Blake said with a sarcastic little laugh. "You've got to be kidding me. Would you listen to him if he asked you to break up with me?"

"That's the difference," I mumbled, pulling the hoodie over my head and marching out the door. "He'd never ask."

Hopping down the stairs, I used my phone as a little flashlight to see where I was stepping. I grabbed the keys before heading out the door, unsure at this point whether or not Blake would even be there when I got back.

Do you want to talk about it? I asked myself. I really didn't.

I turned my music up so loud I could barely think and headed for the one bar that was most likely to be Jace's last stop on a big night out.

By the time I got there, it had long since closed. I went to the glass front door and tried to scan the inside. There were two bartenders in the process of closing up and both of them saw me but made no effort to come over. I knocked on the door as gently as I could, hoping that it would convince them I wasn't a sad drunk or psychotic murderer. Neither of them budged.

I knocked a few more times before a very large and very annoyed man appeared out of the darkness on the other side.

"We're closed!" he yelled. "Go home!"

"I'm looking for my friend. I'm not drunk," I offered, immediately regretting it. It did sound like something someone who was drunk would say to convince others he wasn't drunk.

"There's nobody here. Go home."

Resigned, I turned away from the door and pulled out my

phone. Still nothing. I mentally ran through the possibilities of who he could have been with if he was having a wild night.

I called Annie.

"Johnny?" she asked, sounding either a little groggy or a little tipsy. "What's going on?"

"Are you with Jace?" I asked.

"No. Why?"

"I can't find him. He's kind of disappeared. I thought maybe you had seen him tonight?"

She started to say something, but hesitated.

"Where was he? I need to know. He could be in trouble."

"A group of us went to get drinks earlier. The Naughty Pig in West Hollywood. That was hours ago though."

"Did he say where he was going afterwards?"

"He acted like he was going home, I swear." I could hear the concern in her voice.

"Okay. Listen, if he calls, let me know."

"Of course."

"Thanks," I said quickly before hanging up and heading back to the car.

I did a quick Internet search for hospitals near West Hollywood and sat back in the seat as I dialed each one. Only one of them was willing to tell me they didn't have a patient by the name of Jason Van Noy when I said I was his husband and worried he was in a car wreck.

Out of options, I started to wander aimlessly toward Beverly Hills and think through any previous scenario in which Jace disappeared. It had happened a few more times than I cared to admit. I thought back to the night I had to go to the hospital after he was found on a hiking trail. If he had decided to go out into the wilderness, there was no way I would find him. Certainly not before he'd probably wind up dead.

As I drove, my phone buzzed in my lap. Jace.

"Hey buddy," I gushed, relieved that this meant at the very least, he was alive. "Where are you?"

"I'm home," he said distantly. "What are you doing up so late?"

"You're not home. Riley called me. We're worried about you. Can you tell me where you are? I'll come get you."

"I don't know where I am."

He didn't sound drunk and it worried me more than if he was.

"What's around you?" I asked, hoping he could give me some kind of point of reference.

"I don't know," he said. In the background, I could hear water. The ocean.

"Are you on the beach?"

"No."

"Just stay where you are. Stay on the phone with me."

"Goodbye, John."

The line went dead and I swiveled around to head toward Torrence. If he had left The Naughty Pig and headed in the direction of water, I had a feeling I knew where I'd be able to find him. I made it to Redondo Beach and parked, rushing quickly to the pier. There was a bar there, Tony's, that was one of our favorite haunts.

I saw someone standing near the water and recognized Jace immediately. Trudging through the sand, I rushed toward him. I hated the ocean at night. During the day the endlessness offered little comfort, but at night, it was absolutely terrifying. Everything from my nightmares always felt right off shore, waiting.

"Hey," I said, exhaling as I jogged closer.

"Hey buddy," he replied, before looking at me like he registered me for the first time. "What are you doing here?"

"I was looking for your dumb ass."

"Why? Am I lost?"

"I don't know," I said, scooting to him. "Are you?"

"I guess so." He turned and looked back over the water.

"What are you doing out here so late?"

"I don't know."

"Let's get you home."

He shrugged in the darkness. "I'm good."

I stood there, debating how to approach it all. He didn't seem despondent or manic in any way. He just stood there. Blank.

"Jason," I said quietly. "Let's go home."

He looped his arm through mine, using my body to hold himself up before turning to look back out at the water. "Isn't it peaceful at night?"

"No," I objected, shifting slightly as he leaned his head down to rest on my shoulder. "Not at all. That's terrifying."

He laughed. "You're crazy. It's so calming. Like beyond us, you know? This ocean has been here millions of years, doing the same thing. The water has been flowing back and forth since there were dinosaurs. Isn't that wild?"

"Riley's worried."

His head snapped in the direction of mine as though it occurred to him for the first time that she would be concerned. "Shit. I thought she was asleep."

"She's called you a million times."

He pulled his arm away from mine to get his phone out of his pocket. "I'm sorry, I must have missed it."

I didn't have anything else to say.

Sighing loudly, he turned to me again. "Okay, come on, let's go."

We pushed our way through the rocky sand as we headed back to the little parking lot on the side of the road. A group of teenagers were screaming and chasing one another down the beach.

When we reached the car, he got in, not saying a word. I wasn't sure if I should try to ask more questions and we rode to his house in silence.

I pulled into the driveway and turned off the car. "Are you okay?"

"I'm fine. I'm sorry you had to get out of bed. Riley shouldn't have called you," he said. There was an edge to his tone that I couldn't understand.

"It's fine."

"My problems aren't your problems. You know that, right?" he said suddenly, running his hands through his hair.

I laughed. "Yeah, they are. That's how friendship works. Everyone needs help sometimes."

"Right," he agreed, leaning back in the seat. "Okay, I'm home. I'm good. I'm so sorry. Please go get some sleep."

"Are you sure you're okay? I asked, still unconvinced.

"Come on," he started, leaning forward in the seat to pull my head close and plant a kiss on my cheek. "I'm good. Love you, buddy."

"I love you too," I offered quietly.

He grinned and it was the first time all night he looked like himself. "I know you do."

I watched him get out of the car and make his way up the driveway. As he unlocked the door he turned back to me and raised his hand in a small wave before he disappeared. It took me no time at all to get back home. I sat in the car for a minute before pulling myself up to the door and back up the stairs to our bedroom.

"Did you find him?" Blake asked as I slipped my pants off.

"Yeah, he's home and fine."

Blake rolled over, unwilling to say anything else.

"There are other spaces that love exists. It's not just friendship and it's not always romantic. But it's there and unexplainable. Jace and I can exist in that space and have other relationships, but he always comes first. He always will. I don't know what else to tell you. We were made for each other. To help each other."

There was silence and I wasn't sure if he was pretending to be asleep to avoid the conversation or if he really had conked back out.

"Get in bed and go to sleep," he replied finally.

Annoyed, I pulled my shirt off and moved to the other side of the bed. Not because he told me to, but because I wanted to. I was exhausted.

The minute my head hit the pillow, I was more awake than I thought possible. Thoughts of Jace's concerned face kept flashing over and over in my mind. What was he doing on the beach? Had he planned to drown that very night?

Looking out over the water, I couldn't imagine what it would take to walk forward and inhale the water, feeling the burn as my lungs filled with water. What would it mean to slowly suffocate?

Blake had been wrong then. *Jace* was the one drowning, not me. I had never planned on drowning trying to save him. I hadn't even noticed that he was dying in front of me. Bit by bit, he drifted further away in the water. I didn't see it then. I missed it all.

"You know it wasn't your fault," Dick said finally at my feet.

The ocean roared in front of us and I squinted in the bright sunlight.

"That's not really true, is it?"

"Maybe it doesn't have to be true. Nothing about Jace was really ever true."

I pulled the notebook out of my bag and flipped through it again. A little paper fell out of the back that I hadn't seen before. Rushing forward, I snatched it before the wind carried it away.

I looked at the image. It was a drawing from Jace. Two otters, floating in the water, holding hands to anchor one another.

That's what we had been for each other—anchors in a lost, codependent state.

"It's okay to let go," Dick said so quietly I could barely hear what he was saying.

"I'm afraid if I let go you'll disappear."

"I might," Dick said, his eyes suddenly wide in realization. "Or I might not. We are connected for life after all. Family lasts forever."

I smiled.

"You're right," I admitted. "We are, I guess. Nothing can change that. I can't seem to erase you, no matter how hard I try."

"Fuck you, Johnny."

I laughed and started back to the sand bank. A seagull rushed around the edge of the water, chasing the waves.

"How far are we going?" Dick asked as he followed.

"Stop asking questions you already know the answer to."

I stopped talking as a group of kids ran past us.

Continuing forward, I trudged along in the sand, feeling the resistance of my feet on the ground beneath me. Dick waddled as quickly as he could to keep up, talking the whole way.

"How does this look?" I asked, scanning the distant pier. From that spot, I could barely make out Tony's.

"Works for me."

He got to work, pulling out his own little beach chair and

umbrella, assembling everything around him in cartoon time. I unfolded my own human-sized chair and pulled my shirt off before settling back to bask in the sun.

"This is the season finale, isn't it?" he asked behind a tiny pair of shades, sipping a crazy straw that was stuck inside a coconut.

"Yeah, I think it is."

I let the wind from the waves push against my face as I closed my eyes and did nothing but feel the warmth of the sun on my cheeks and inhale the comfort of the salty air, feeling alive for the first time in months. *Goodbye, my friend. I'll miss you always.*

"What's it going to be—cliffhanger for season two? Dramatic emotional resolution? Happily ever after?"

"I don't know. All of the above?" I asked, folding my arms behind my head in the chair. "I doubt we'll get a season two, to be honest. Doesn't really seem like there's a market for it."

"Rude."

"How do you want to end?"

"I've never really thought about it."

I laughed. "That's a lie. We think about it all the time."

"Well, you've got to give me time to think of a final line."

"Says who?"

"Those are the rules. It can't end like that—with us talking about the finale. That meta-shit is over played."

"Then you better think fast."

"No, come on, these are not my—

END.

ACKNOWLEDGMENTS

Where do we begin?

I want to take a minute to thank my family for all of their support in my life. Mom and Dad—I'm so grateful for you encouraging me to think up little goofy stories and fostering my love of all forms of story telling. My brothers—Jeff, Chris, Brady—thank you for everything; also Megan, Thomas, Lucy and Lois—I love you all.

Jessica—you are the origin of this entire story. Our singular conversation that one night sparked the whole world of my sarcastic animated duck marred in the mess of mental illness and despair. Thank you for the support, encouragement, editing, and all manner of tasks you've taken on as my unofficial writing manager.

To all of my friends that believed in Dick from the very beginning—Brittany and Chelsea in particular—thank you for your constant support. I'd be lost without you.

To the best beta reader in the world—Zachary—I'm grateful for your honesty and your notes.

To Kristina, thank you for being willing to take on my dark, weird little mind and champion this story in the way I felt it always deserved. To my editor, Tasha, thank you for believing in Dick from the beginning. To everyone at Truborn Press, I'm so grateful for the chance I was given to present this story.

To everyone who bought this book—thank you for your support of me and of small presses. I appreciate your investment into my words and hope they can be used for forces of good in a world that tries so hard sometimes to tear us down. Thank you for supporting queer writers and queer stories.

It's not goodbye, little bird, it's only until you turn the next page. Much love.

ABOUT THE AUTHOR

Samantha Ryan is a queer writer from Tulsa, Oklahoma. She has a chunky German Shepherd named Harley, an incredibly needy cat named Baxter, and half a dozen plants she can barely keep alive.

For more information, check out samryanreally.com

PREVIOUS PUBLICATIONS

- Pride [*Rattling Good Yarns Press*]
- Words My Friends Have Thrown Away [*SIAMB!*]

A NOTE FROM TRUBORN PRESS

We want to thank our readers for their support and enthusiasm. Your passion for stories fuels our commitment to bring you the horror that is strange and horrifying in the best of ways.

We appreciate any and all reviews, so help us out by leaving your thoughts online.

Thank you again for spending your time with us and remember to...

Follow us everywhere: @trubornpress
Subscribe to our newsletter today!
www.trubornpress.com

CONTENT NOTES

- Mental Illness
- Suicide
- Grief
- Disordered Eating
- Death